Praise for Tony Tremblay:

"Tony's writing will fill any horror reader's appetite - rest assured."
~ Jeff Kivela - Buttonholed Book Reviews

THE MOORE HOUSE

"I'm a big fan of religious-themed horror, and I enjoyed Tremblay's approach. With plenty of haunted house mayhem, an interesting cast, and a flawed but likable crew of demon hunters...a fine debut and a quick read to get the chills going."
~ The Horror Fiction Review

"I adored this horror novel, in every sense. Author Tony Tremblay knows how to terrorize his characters and his readers. I read this over two evenings/nights, which was really brave of me since **THE MOORE HOUSE** is super scary. I won't be forgetting this novel for quite a long time. I especially won't forget the explosively terrifying opening scenes involving a homeless, feckless, drifter--and THE MOORE HOUSE."
~ The Haunted Reading Room

"...an unrelenting tale of possession, distantly echoing themes of The Amityville Horror, The Exorcist, and Poltergeist. From the opening page the reader is pulled into the fictional hell of Tony's mind, and it doesn't stop until the final pages. There is no fat on this book - it is lean and muscled, at times brutally graphic. ...this treasure was devoured within two days. Not because it's an easy read, but rather the almost seamless and unpretentious style in which Tony writes."
~ Michael Upstill's Reviews

BLUE STARS

"...hits a reader in a dark, visceral, deeply emotional place. It's not a book where one might seek classical prose or avant-garde rhythm and imagery. This is one-on-one, intimate storytelling — a writer spinning a yarn to punch you right smack in the gut, rather than challenge the more clinical, rational centers of the brain.
~ Stephen Mark Rainey, author of BLUE DEVIL ISLAND -

THE SEEDS OF NIGHTMARES

"A new, confident voice breaks out with a first collection of stories that leaves space for empathy and humanity between the horrors. It's very obvious the writer has read an enormous amount - which of course all writers should - and absorbed the lessons of many masters. Looking forward to future work from a writer who is not "up and coming" but has arrived, right here and now!"

~ Gerard Houarner, author of SLEEPERS

"...a smorgasbord – a feast of emotions and genres that cover the spectrum. Take his opening offering for example, the nasty little novelette The Strange Saga of Mattie Dyer, a darkly humorous, Lovecraftian, western, tale of vengeance (yes, you read that right). Wrought with unsavory and despicable characters—a thwarted woman, a vile creature, redneck gold-diggers, and Indians—it's a virtual Pandora's Box and a hell of a first run…. There will be twists, bumps, a little blood, and possibly a few tears, but you're tough…you can take it. So have a seat, strap in, and enjoy the ride!"

~ John McIlveen, bestselling author of HANNAHWHERE

DO NOT WEEP FOR ME

TONY TREMBLAY

An imprint of
Haverhill House Publishing

978-1-949140-11-8 (Hardcover)
978-1-949140-30-9 (Trade Paperback)

First Edition

Twisted Publishing is an imprint of
Haverhill House Publishing LLC

For more information, address:

Haverhill House Publishing
643 E Broadway
Haverhill MA 01830-2420

Visit us on the web at www.HaverhillHouse.com

Dedicated to
Anthony Tremblay and Laura Tremblay

ACKNOWLEDGMENTS

Thanks to my wife, my son and his family, and my daughter and her family for keeping me grounded while this novel was in progress. Thanks to Linda Nagle for an exceptional job on the major edits for *Do Not Weep for Me*, and to David Dodd for providing the final edits. Thanks are also in order to The Blank Page and The Goffstown NH Public Library. While none of these characters are based on real people, I did use the names of my friends for some of the characters. I am grateful for these friends; I hope I honor them with the name-dropping. A generous smile, a tip of the hat, and a friendly shout out goes to Nanci Kalanta and all my Horror World friends, Necon, NoCon, and Facebook friends. You guys keep me going. You guys keep me writing. Saving the best for last, I want to thank John McIlveen...for everything.

ONE

The Subaru Outback swerved to the right, scraped the curb, and crossed the solid yellow line. The grind of metal on metal cut the silence of evening as the Outback sideswiped two parked cars and clipped the Lions Club popcorn stand. Far from a smooth maneuver, the driver pulled the vehicle into its final destination—a paved parking lot. Tires squealed as she applied the brakes in a bid not to overshoot the space. The front wheels bounced over a concrete stop and came to a halt, the bumper overhanging the sidewalk.

The Outback was the only car in the Goffstown Hardware parking lot. With no idea of the time, or even the day, the voice in her head assured her it was early evening on a Sunday. The vacant lot was a matter of good fortune.

Something pressed her body tight against the seat. Damp fingers slipped from the steering wheel and folded upon her lap. Pressure beneath her chin lifted her gaze until her eyes were level with the center of the windshield. Her neck muscles bulged as she surveyed the building across the street. Large plate-glass windows framed the exterior, bracketing a set of double doors. The glass was tinted enough to prevent light from seeping through in either direction. That same assuring voice in her head said she wouldn't be able to stand outside and look through the windows before entering. *An advantage lost,* it added.

1

A weathered awning hung above the double doors; block letters read GOFFSTOWN PAWN SHOP. In a portion of her mind of which she retained *some* control, she questioned why anyone would go through the expense of installing secure, high-quality windows and doors yet use a stained and worn sign for advertising their business. A pair of red dots glowed, one on either side of the awning. *Cameras.* She managed one more follow-up thought before her reasoning clouded—*why does a pawnshop need to be so well-protected?*

A tug at her shoulders set her in motion. Unlocking the seatbelt, she pulled on the door handle. She leaned into it, pushing it open all the way. The car was a late-model, well-kept—no squeaking of hinges or grinding sounds announced her extraction from the vehicle. Holding on to the doorframe, she steadied herself. A breeze fluttered her dress. Warm, damp fecal matter slid down her legs and onto the pavement. She had driven from Colby, Kansas, twenty-nine hours without a bathroom break. Pausing only to gas up outside of Columbus at a highway Burger King, she had purchased food and coffee at the drive-up. The demon wanted her awake, so aside from that sole stop, it had forced her to punch herself in the face whenever she exhibited signs of fatigue. Though her nose was broken, the demon controlled her pain so she could function. After steadying herself against the door, her focus shifted to the back seat of the car.

The remains of a young woman and her adolescent daughter lay decomposing under a blue plastic tarp. The rear seats were folded down to make room for both bodies. Blood pooled on the floor beneath them. Not all of it had dried. Forbidden to turn on the air conditioner or roll down the windows, the driver had had no choice but to put up with the stench during her journey to Goffstown. Memories pulled at her, fighting through the cloud in her mind.

In a city park outside Colby, she crept up to the pair. A knife she had stolen from a dead trucker whose rig idled at the other side of the park was held tight behind her back. Though she had approached from behind, the mother's intuition must have sensed her. Adjusting her child's backpack, the mother swung around to face her aggressor and sprang into action. There was no time to flee, so she wrapped her arms around her daughter, pulling her close.

Her memories clearer, she saw herself advance on the mother and child.

She wasted no time. The trucker's knife plunged into the mother's right breast. Her lips parted, a groan escaped. She released the child, and her hands went to the handle. Too weak to pull it out, her hands dropped. Her knees buckled and her legs crumpled. She lay on her back as red foam bubbled from her lips. The mother whispered, implored her daughter to run. The young girl ignored the order, throwing herself beside the dying woman. Her mother's pleas, weak, almost inaudible, had no effect. "Run, Jasmine, run...." The child cradled her mother's head, begging her to get up.

As she recalled the scene, the demon inside her gloated. Following the trail of blood from the woman's chest to the ground, she wondered what her last thoughts had been. Did she beg God for help? When none arrived, did she plead for forgiveness? Had this woman ever cheated on her husband? Beat the child?

The demon inside her had cared nothing for such concerns. It desired only that the woman would live for a few moments longer—so she could watch her daughter die.

It got its way.

An image of herself bending over at the waist, hovering above the mother, now came to her. Reaching down, she pulled. The serrated knife slid from the woman's wound with little resistance.

Delighting in the memory, the demon twisted the woman's mouth into a grin as she recalled how tender the flesh of the young girl's neck was. *The mother's eyes widened. Before clouding over, the woman focused on something only she could see. With a heavy breath, the mother followed her daughter into the next world.*

Having ceded control of her will well before this event, the demon had forced her to stand over the mother and daughter as they had breathed their last. The demon relished the deaths. It had granted her a moment's lucidity so it could revel in her agony.

Free of the demon's oppression, she silently screamed. The mother couldn't have been much older than her mid-thirties. Her child might have reached the fifth grade. The demon reclaimed her, stressing she was the reason they were dead. The smile on her face and the sparkle in her eyes masked the chaos in her head. That smile never left her lips as she placed the bodies into the mother's Outback.

With a snap of her neck, the demon brought her back to the present.

The driver turned her focus back to the pawnshop. Her grip slipped from the doorframe, and she stepped away. Leaning back against the hood, her fists opened, closed, and opened again. A burning sensation in her fingers claimed her attention. The nails on both hands had changed. They had thickened, grown at least two inches, the tips coming to a point.

The demon judged her ready.

4

"Hey, Rex, stop what you're doing, come here a minute."

The pawnshop owner's assistant stood in the middle of the shop floor. In his hands, held waist-high, was a three-hundred-pound stone. He lowered it, taking care not to crack the cement floor or damage the housing crate. In a voice as abrasive as 60 grit sandpaper, Rex asked, "What's in this?"

"It's supposed to be a scrying stone—a divining mirror. A sorcerer by the name of John Dee built it in 1590."

Rex responded with a noncommittal grunt.

The pawnshop owner had taken possession of the relic via a commission purchase for a customer who had authenticated it and advanced the payment. Aside from its purported clairvoyant prowess and the myths that accompanied it, another oddity surrounded the object—it should not have been there. It was reportedly housed in a British museum. Google confirmed its location, which left the pawnshop owner with a number of questions. Was the one in his shop a fake, or was the one in the museum the forgery? Could there be two of them? Though he did love a mystery, this one had little to do with him, so he brushed the conundrum aside.

A forklift had offloaded the crate from a flatbed truck earlier that afternoon, and it sat by the front doors until his assistant arrived. Rex, weighing over four hundred pounds and with a physique reminiscent of a bull, spent little effort lifting and placing the crate in the middle of the shop floor. Rex had no impediments when he carried it inside; the area was wide open—all the merchandise for sale or display was stored on racks against the four walls. Apart from those racks, a long counter running close to the west wall also claimed a sliver of floor space, giving a first impression to anyone entering the pawnshop that the place was almost empty. Rex swiveled his head around to face the owner and asked, "Where do you want this?"

Pointing, the pawnshop owner answered, "Against the far wall, in that space open between those two racks. It should fit." He was not surprised that the brute didn't offer so much as a grunt while carrying the stone. After the task was complete, Rex joined him at the counter, where he was looking at a video screen.

"Rex, the motion detector flashed, so I thought I'd take a look at the camera feed. She's been out there leaning against that car for a few minutes now, staring at our front doors. What do you think?"

Rex was tall enough to look over the owner's shoulder, but he bent down to study the screen. As he evaluated the feed, his heavy breathing warmed the pawnshop owner's neck.

The shop owner ignored the intermittent blasts of hot breath and waited patiently for an evaluation.

After a long pause, Rex answered.

"Her head jerks occasionally. Same with her hands. I've seen her knees buckle, but she recovers fast. Her hair is stringy, greasy, sticking to the side of her head. The dress, stained. There's shit running down her leg. A car passed slowly, but she didn't take her eyes off the front doors." He grew quiet, then added, "Drug addict?"

The pawnshop owner stepped to the side, did a one-eighty, and faced Rex. "Her appearance and tics dictate prudence. I'm going to secure the shop."

Rex nodded, and they both returned their attention to the screen.

The woman was gone. Confused, the pawnshop owner hesitated before acting.

The double doors flew open.

The sound boomed through the pawnshop, and the owner cursed. He had waited too long. He should have pressed one of the buttons recessed in the counter that automatically secured the shop. Behind him, he heard Rex utter a gravelly, "Fuck".

The woman stood in the doorway.

The pawnshop owner kept his eyes on her. "Rex, please go around and stand at the other side of the counter."

The giant issued a soft grunt and did as he was told.

In the doorway, the woman's head trembled as she surveyed the pawnshop. Swaying and off-balance, her arms flailed to keep her centered. The woman's eyes were wide, black as charcoal, and she was staring up at a shelf behind the pawnshop owner.

He flinched. *Shit, she knows about the Prexy Box.*

The woman lowered her head and stepped forward.

For someone so gangly, the woman had no difficulty crossing the distance between the doors and the counter. Her steps were light and made no sound, as though her feet glided over the cement rather than making contact. She halted a foot before the counter.

The pawnshop owner leaned back and studied the woman. Pits on her face trickled a dark yellow fluid. Blood dribbled from cracked, bleeding lips, staining her chin. Her nose was shifted to one side—dark patches surrounding it highlighted the severity of the bruising. An unexpected smile revealed chipped teeth. A blistered tongue teased at them while her gaze returned to the shelf above him.

"Mr. Smith, you have something we need," she said.

The proprietor stiffened.

Mr. Smith was a name he had proffered only once. Pressured to reveal it to a priest, he had responded with the most generic name he could think of. Names were powerful. In the wrong hands, they could lead to devastating consequences. That one time he had used *Mr. Smith*, he was battling two demons at a local home called the Moore House. He had come out on the winning side of that confrontation and believed the situation had been resolved permanently.

Visions of what had occurred inside that house clouded his thoughts. Most of them hinged on Celeste, an excommunicated nun who had saved his life that day by allowing one of the demons to possess her and then trapping it inside her soul. She remained comatose; that same priest was still working to exorcise the demon from her. Celeste's plight had weighed heavy on him since.

"Mr. Smith, you can give me the box, or I can take it." The woman's voice commanded his attention. He shook off the images of the Moore House and placed his hands on the counter without taking his eyes off her. He took a few moments before replying.

"This innocent woman you've inhabited, is she lost?"

"Yes." A pause, then, "She is not so innocent."

At that moment, the woman's face changed. The darkness in her eyes faded, a light sheen with a hint of blue reflected back at him. The intensity in her stare telegraphed fear, only to soften an instant later into clouds of resignation. She blinked, and when her eyes reopened, they were black once again.

The pawnshop owner pitied the soul trapped by this demon. Though he did not know how she had come to be possessed, he understood her time on earth was done. Her next life would be one of unspeakable pain and horror. Taking a breath, he nodded to Rex, who returned the gesture.

The pawnshop owner pressed down his right middle finger into a recess on the counter.

The shop floor began to rumble, and overhead, turning gears and spinning pulleys thundered. Flashes of light reflected off unseen objects as they crashed down from the ceiling. Thick, translucent panels fell into place in front of the counter, racks, doors, and windows. The pawnshop was contained. No one could access what was behind the counter or leave the shop. Those trapped inside the transparent prison were restricted to the open floor. Etched into the panels were runes—an assist to compromise the power of a supernatural entity further.

The possessed woman did not react in surprise or panic. Instead, she studied the barrier between herself and the pawnshop owner and placed her palms against it. Instinct pushed the proprietor to step back.

The flesh on the woman's hands reddened, bubbled. Wisps of white smoke rose upon contact. Her expression evidenced no pain. Head cocked to the side, she noted how they burned and jerked her arm in an attempt to remove her hands from the barrier. Her palms stuck, and the wisps of smoke thickened, grew darker. Leaning back, she tried again.

The shop owner's eyes widened at her success. Two handprints, the remnants of scorched skin, floated in the space between them. The woman smiled.

She stepped forward, halting when her nose contacted the transparent barrier. Her face erupted in blisters as her arms rose above her head. Her fingers curled, forming claws. White smoke spiraled to the ceiling as she placed the pointed tips of her nails against the panel. As she lowered her hands, scratches materialized on the translucent panel.

When her hands could go no lower, she lifted them and repeated the act, following the path of the original scratches. They became deeper.

The pawnshop owner searched the countertop for a second recessed button. Finding it, his voice boomed from the speaker inside the sealed-off area. In a calm voice, he said, "Rex, she's going to break through."

There was no acknowledgment.

Rex took a step forward.

The possessed woman's dark eyes remained on the pawnshop owner as she pawed and scraped at the panel. She was unaware of the giant's presence when he slipped behind her.

Rex raised his hands, extended them over the woman's head, and brought them down like hammers on her arms.

Her claws ripped from the panel. The bones in her arms should have been shattered, but it didn't happen. There was no blood, no white protruding through her flesh. Instead, her arms swung behind her and she dug her claws into the giant's thighs.

Blood ran as her nails ripped through flesh.

Rex stood two feet taller than the woman, so the pawnshop owner had no trouble seeing his assistant's face grimace in pain. A scowl, born of anger, took its place. Rex pulled the woman's arms away from his thighs. Ten red stains materialized on the man's cargo pants, and seconds later, they expanded into massive blotches. Rex held the woman's arms high, blood dripped from her hands onto his head and shoulders. Crimson streaked his face, highlighting eyes that burned with fury.

Rex pulled the woman from off the floor. It took only seconds to lift her above his head. With a grunt, he sent her airborne toward the far end of the shop.

The woman never hit the wall. She froze in mid-air before impact—motionless like a snapshot, fixed above the floor. Her lifeless eyes locked on a shelf behind the pawnshop owner.

Seconds passed, no one moved.

The strange woman broke the impasse. She jerked her head toward them, an inch at a time. Seeing Rex, her lips parted. Yellowed teeth chattered. The woman's lower body angled down and dropped. As her feet landed on the floor, she started clicking her teeth. Eyes wide and black, arms extended with nails dripping blood, she advanced toward the giant.

Hands curled into fists, Rex barreled forward, rushing her.

She was ready for him.

Rex let his left arm fly and the woman leaned away from the blow. His fist flew through the gap between them, but before his swing was complete, she grabbed his wrist. Forward momentum left no chance for his body to slow down. With incredible speed, she swiveled behind him.

Not only did her feet remain planted on the floor, but she was also coordinated enough to push off. She leaped onto his back. Her arms swung around his neck, and she gripped his torso between her thighs.

One of her hands released its grip on the giant's neck and she raked her pointed nails across his face.

Rex growled loud enough to be heard through the barrier.

Though the growl was unsettling, a sense of ease befell the pawnshop owner. He had heard this before. His assistant had had enough.

Rex squatted.

Pushing off with his legs, he leaped high into the air. The giant came down on his back. Four hundred pounds of muscle slammed the woman's body against the floor. Blood and piss-yellow fluid pooled beneath their bodies.

Neither he nor the woman moved.

The pawnshop owner scanned the countertop and pressed the microphone button. "Rex, are you okay?"

Rex sat up. Beneath him, the woman remained still, soaked in a puddle of her bodily fluids. As he stood, he made eye contact with the pawnshop owner and nodded. The big man's attention went to the body on the floor.

The pawnshop owner couldn't decide if Rex was curious or admiring his kill. *Whatever you do, Rex, don't move any closer.*

The woman shot up.

In the blink of an eye, she was on her feet. Spine crushed, her upper body leaned at an odd angle, her pelvis jutting to the left. Bulges in her neck indicated broken bones. Without support, her head wobbled from side to side, up and down, and her tongue lolled. Her limbs did not appear to be damaged. Her arms were extended like wings, her hands outstretched.

The woman lunged. Razor-sharp nails hit their target, and the talons plunged into Rex's chest.

Rex let out another roar. He lifted his arms and placed both hands at the sides of the woman's head. His massive fingers clamped around her skull, and with a grunt, he pulled upward. Her skin stretched. Her neck lengthened. He pulled harder. Flesh tore. With a squish, the woman's head separated from her neck and her body collapsed to the floor.

The giant held the head high above him. With a scowl, he stared at it. "Fuck you."

"*No, fuck you,*" it replied.

Rex dropped the head and stumbled back.

The pawnshop owner reached into the recess in the counter and pressed. The building shook as the groans of wheels and pulleys bounced off the retracting translucent panels. When the shop was quiet, he made his way around the counter and stood next to Rex. Both men fixated on the decapitated head. The black void in the woman's eyes was fading. As she blinked a hint of blue appeared.

"You have my army in your box, Mr. Smith. I will be back."

The pawnshop owner shuddered. With her throat shredded, she should not have been able to speak.

The head closed its eyes. Upon reopening, it seemed from the color of her eyes the woman's soul was reemerging. The pawnshop owner refused to take pity on her. "How did this happen to you?"

She licked her lips. *"I played at being a witch. I read Tarot cards, employed Ouija boards, and sought out books of magic. I acquired The Lesser Key of Solomon, and believing I could control it, I conjured a demon."*

He sneered. "How'd that work out for you?"

"This is not the way I thought I would die."

The eyes were black once more. The demon's voice was low, distant, threatening. *"Give me the box."*

The pawnshop owner pointed at the head. "Rex, please take care of that."

Rex took a step forward. He lifted his right foot and brought all his weight down. There was no way of knowing what color its eyes were now. "It said you had its army. What did it mean?"

He sighed. "I believe it was referring to the souls residing in the Prexy Box."

It was Rex's turn to sigh.

TWO

The sidewalk in front of the *Goffstown Times* had turned grainy and faded to a dark gray long ago. Weeds inhabited cracks and the dirt-filled holes with foot traffic ensured their stunted growth. The remnants of junk-food wrappers and the odd blackened penny co-existed on the worn blacktop claiming homesteading rights. The sidewalk's neglect mirrored the frontage of the building. The brickwork was in severe need of pointing and so old that Manuel Chance, the owner of the newspaper, would be hard-pressed to recall the wall's deep red façade. An older woman with a slight hump on her back limped past the front of the building and he could not help but compare her to the condition of the sidewalk.

Over the past two weeks, Manuel had watched the woman shuffle past his plate-glass window at least a dozen times. Her straight, long, and unkempt hair matched the color of the faded walkway. Her face had more worry lines and wrinkles than the sidewalk had cracks. Her poor posture—all angles, with the left shoulder preceding the right by a few inches— was more noticeable due to the hump and the concaveness in the small of her back. There was also the limp. Her body leaned to the side with every left step, then straightened briefly as her right leg took its turn. Thinking her gait resembled a wobble, Manuel nicknamed her Duck Lady.

Duck Lady's pattern of walking by with hardly a sidelong glance was broken when she paused at the midpoint of the window. She turned and peered in at Manuel.

He was sitting at his desk, staring out at Main Street while trying to decide if a broken water main on Spring Street was worthy of inclusion in this week's paper, when Duck Lady diverted his attention. Though he could not recall having seen the woman before these past two weeks, something about her was familiar. As he tried to remember, he smiled and nodded at her, as a good townie should. Expecting dismissal, or a disinterested smile at best, his curiosity was piqued when she cocked her head and studied him further. They appraised each other. She backed up, stepped to the storefront entrance, and wobbled in. Though it was early August and quite warm, the woman was dressed head to toe in black, her ankle-length dress skimming the tops of her shoes. Duck Lady inched to Manuel's desk as slowly as she had walked past his window. It gave him a chance to study her eyes for the first time. Though half-open, they were ashen, lacked fire, and appeared glazed with a matte varnish. If she had trouble seeing, it was not apparent; she focused on him like a cat pondering a mouse playing dead.

Manuel remained quiet until Duck Lady stood before his desk. The odor of burned oak with a whisper of pine filled his nostrils.

He stood to greet her. "Can I help you, Ma'am?"

Before answering, she regarded him carefully. Satisfied, she asked, "Are you Manuel Chance?" Her strong voice belied her appearance. It made him pause before replying.

"You know my name, but it seems I am at a disadvantage."

"Mr. Chance. Could I trouble you for a chair and a moment of your time?"

"Of course."

Manuel grabbed a chair and slid it to the front of his desk.

As the woman sat, she breathed a sigh. "Thank you."

Manuel nodded and returned to his side of the desk. He sat, leaned back, and waited for her to speak.

"My name is Irene Delaney."

He straightened up. "You—you were the woman kidnapped last year?" Irene Delaney had been 42 at the time; this woman appeared to be in her mid-sixties.

"Yes, that was me."

Taken by four men from a neighboring town, Delaney was missing for four months. Details about the case were scarce, to protect the woman's privacy. Manuel recalled she had somehow escaped her captors. The police discovered all four men dead at the site of her confinement; the case remained open, but Manuel doubted much effort was spent on it.

The *Goffstown Times* naturally covered the story, but it was mostly a rehash or reprints from other news sources. His was a weekly one-person newspaper with a disdain for publishing gossip and innuendo, and which relied on stringers who provided content to fill the pages. Consequently, when the case was stalled, and the news flow stopped, he, too, let the story die.

Since this was Goffstown, there was always some horrendous news story to occupy the townspeople. Before Delaney's abduction, the Moore House had burned down, revealing it as the site of ritualistic murders. Recently, four children had disappeared from their homes. The missing children were the hot news-*du jour*.

"I'm very sorry you went through that ordeal, Mrs. Delaney. I can't begin to imagine what it must have been like."

The woman shook her head. "No, you can't, Mr. Chance, but I would like to give you some idea."

Manuel's eyes widened. "Are you here to give me the details of your kidnapping? Is this something you want me to print?"

Mrs. Delaney shifted in her chair. "Yes and no. I would like to discuss with you what happened, but only because it relates to the reason I came here to speak to you. I've debated for weeks how much to share with you, and I came to the conclusion that I should tell you everything. I'm still unsure—I almost walked past your office again just now, but I need to do this if I am to have any peace. I will give you my story, Mr. Chance. However, I have one stipulation."

"Go on."

The woman lowered her eyes. "I want it off the record, for now."

"I don't understand."

"I want you to investigate something that might be related to what those men did to me. It has to do with the missing children. If you agree to help me, we can discuss how much you can print."

Manuel sat back. This woman's story was every reporter's dream. It would dwarf anything the *Goffstown Times* had ever run, and he would be scooping New Hampshire's statewide daily newspaper. Images of advertisers' checks played before his eyes. Reflecting on it further, he felt his enthusiasm dampen. *What if this woman is crazy?* She had gone through one hell of an ordeal—her physical appearance bore that out. Could the kidnapping have affected her mental stability? Would he be wasting his time chasing her delusions? If her story about the missing kids did have merit, would he be placing himself in the middle of a police investigation? More disturbing, would he be putting himself in harm's way?

"Mrs. Delaney, shouldn't you be going to the police with your suspicions?"

"No. If my suspicions are wrong, I would be placing an innocent man under unwarranted scrutiny. That would not be justice, nor would it be morally correct. I need someone with no bias to evaluate my suspicions and either support my assumptions or put them to rest."

"No bias? Who do you believe might be involved in taking these missing children?"

"Donald. My husband."

Manuel's mouth dropped. He didn't know her husband that well, mostly from only having spotted him around town. The closest interaction he'd had with the man was when he had seen him one evening at the local scum bar. Manuel, a bachelor, occasionally went there after work for a beer before heading home to dinner. One evening, when Mrs. Delaney was still missing, he saw her husband there. Mr. Delaney was slurring, staggering around, asking fellow pub goers if they had seen his wife. While Manuel observed from the safety of the bar, a group of young men at a nearby table teased the man about his missing wife. A struggle broke out, during which Mr. Delaney got the worst of it. At one point, Mr. Delaney caught Manuel's eye and silently pleaded for help. Manuel wanted no part of the fight and refused to intervene.

The confrontation didn't last all that long. Lifted by the four men and tossed outside the front door, Mr. Delaney did not return for any more punishment. Manuel had sympathy for the man, but not enough to take on a bunch of goons who looked like motorcycle gang members.

"Mrs. Delaney, what evidence do you have that your husband may be connected to the missing children?"

She lifted her chin. "I have my suspicions based on his comments. You need to come to my house and see if there *is* any."

"What about your husband?"

"You should come while he is at work."

Alarm bells went off in Manuel's head. Was she setting him up? If so, why? "I'm not all that comfortable visiting your home while your husband is at work. May I bring someone along?"

The woman leaned forward and stared at him. "I understand why you would feel uncomfortable being alone with a married woman in her home, Mr. Chance. The answer is no. The fewer people who are aware of my suspicions at this time, the better. If you are refusing my offer as it stands, I will be on my way." She leaned to the right, adjusting her body so she could put more weight onto the armrest. She pushed with her right hand, and, with some effort, stood. Her eyes never left him.

"Mrs. Delaney, you should go to the police with this. I'm sure they will be discreet."

She leaned down to him. "The police are competent, but the department is small. They had four months to find me. You have no idea how many times they came close but missed the opportunity to save me. You don't know this, Mr. Chance, but the four men who kidnapped me beat my husband one night when he was at a bar. My husband reported the incident to the police, and nothing came of it. He told me what happened, how nobody would help him."

Manuel's spine stiffened, and he lowered his head.

"Because of that beating, my husband found me a week later. Those four men had taunted him while they beat him.

Days later, my husband remembered that one of the men said something odd. While the man was choking my husband, he asked my husband if he missed his wife's shaved pussy. It so happens that I do shave my private parts, Mr. Chance. Of course, it could have been a childish taunt, but once my husband remembered it, it wouldn't leave his head."

"Did he tell the police?"

The woman nodded. "Yes, but again, nothing came of it. He decided to take matters into his own hands. My husband tracked down those four men. He was the one who found me, Mr. Chance, not law enforcement. He saw what they did to me, and he hasn't been the same since."

"What did they do to you?" Manuel whispered.

Mrs. Delaney hobbled to the plate-glass window and drew the blind, and then her hands went to her waist. She pulled at her dress, gathering up the material. When the hem reached her waist, she lifted higher and pulled the dress up and over her head. She placed it on the chair.

Manuel swallowed hard and gritted his teeth. He shook his head.

Her skin had been used as a canvas.

From the bottom of Mrs. Delaney's neck to just above her ankles were tattoos, so numerous and dense only the barest of pink flesh was visible. Every tattoo was black with a combination of letters and symbols, none of which made sense or were familiar to him. Her arms from the wrists up were the same. Unlike her face, the inked skin was tight against her lean frame.

"My God."

Mrs. Delaney squinted. "God had nothing to do with this, Mr. Chance."

"I—I'm sorry...." His voice trailed off.

"They not only desecrated my body, they altered it. I was strapped down over a thin, filthy mattress for four months. They placed a solid, half-round sphere under the mattress. It pressed against my back, altering it, distorting my body. Being forced into that position was more painful than the needles. What those men did to me was evil, Mr. Chance, and I'm reminded of it every day of my life." She lifted the dress off the chair and put it back on.

Manuel lowered his head and ran his fingers through his hair. This woman had already been through so much, and her ordeal might not be over. Was she feeling a sense of guilt or complicity if her husband did kidnap those children? Manuel's gut told him to stay away and not have anything to do with her. She was damaged, and damaged people were not to be trusted. She claimed she was trying to find out if her husband was guilty, but for what reason? Was it to prevent further abductions? Did she plan to turn him in? Or was she attempting to protect him by having someone look for obvious clues, and then she would destroy the evidence? Still, she appeared sincere. She said she wanted to tell her story once she found the truth, and, she didn't have to show him what those bastards had done to her. It was one hell of a story, though, one that could benefit him in many ways. He would have to think it through.

When she finished dressing, she asked, "What do you say, Mr. Chance? Are you going to assist me?"

"You will give me the complete story? Not only of what happened to you but if I discover that your husband has something to do with the missing children, that I'll be able to write about that, too?"

"Yes. But, if we find out that my husband had nothing to do with the abductions, you are not to mention that portion of the story."

Manuel nodded. "Okay, Mrs. Delaney, I'll work with you."

The woman let out a sigh. "I will call you tomorrow. I will leave the details on your voicemail if you are not here. Thank you, Mr. Chance, for assisting me."

Mrs. Delaney left the office. He expected her to walk past the plate-glass window, allowing him one more look. Instead, she turned right out the door.

THREE

Paul Lane glanced at the thermometer on his front porch—74 degrees—and then, cup of coffee in hand, stood on the concrete steps. He noted the thick cloud cover. Its gray hue muted the sunshine, dulling the vibrant palette of the season. He looked down and frowned. The grass covering his yard looked different. The stiff, neatly-trimmed blades rested limply on the topsoil. The deep shamrock green had faded, its tips tinged with yellow. *Too tired-looking for mid-June.*

The flowers on the Rose of Sharon hedge, so proud yesterday, were now listless. Their parade of bright red blossoms absorbed the muted sunlight and reflected a color more akin to copper than candy apple.

The neighborhood had taken on a dingy appearance. It was as if the brick, aluminum, and vinyl siding façades on the homes had bathed in a layer of dust. Not one of the new cars screamed, "Look at me." Their wax jobs lacked sparkle, their chrome trims dull.

Something was off.

People in his neighborhood had pride. They were not known for neglecting their property.

"Daddy?"

The call broke his concentration. "Yes, Cindy?"

"Can I play on the swing for a few minutes before you take me to school?"

Paul didn't answer. There was a heaviness to the area he couldn't put his finger on: the atmosphere had weight. Not only was it oppressive, it was concerning in a way that defied easy description.

He caught sight of Sheila White, the neighbor across the street, as she retrieved the daily newspaper from the box at the end of her driveway. The woman waved to him, and he waved back. She was a fine-looking woman and knew it. He smiled when she stopped a few feet from her front door and wiggled her ass before stepping back inside. Paul's wife had been dead for four years now, but that didn't mean he was. Though Sheila often flirted with him, she was off limits. He and her husband, Tom, were good friends, and he would never betray that trust. Still, she did brighten Paul's mood on occasion.

"Daddy, can I?"

"Huh?" He had forgotten about Cindy. "Yeah, sure, honey. Stay in the back. I'll come get you when it's time to leave. You want to eat anything before you have breakfast at daycare?"

"No. I'm okay. Can you push me?"

He chuckled. "Sure. Give me a minute to bring my stuff to the car. I'll be right out."

"Thanks, Daddy!" She gave him a quick hug and ran back inside.

He followed her in and, after chugging his coffee, Paul draped his suit coat over his arm and grabbed his briefcase and backpack. There was a *thud*, confirming his daughter had gone through the back door to get to the swing set. The forecast promised clear weather, so he'd left his car in the driveway overnight. He walked to the Lexus with thoughts of that morning's meeting he had planned with his company's engineers. He made a mental note to review the cost analysis on the retrofit of the South Willow Street strip mall in Manchester. Lost in thought, he threw his suit coat and briefcase into the rear seat. After shutting the door, he made an effort to clear his head and attend to Cindy. He walked past an area of tall pines and scrub that marked the property line on the right side of his house. When he was about to turn the corner to the back yard, he slowed.

This doesn't feel right.

He should have heard squeaks from the rusty chains attached to the joints at the top of the swing set. He'd meant to oil them but had never found the time. The squeaks were annoyingly loud; you could hear them from twenty feet away. His back stiffened and he hurried his pace.

She could be sitting and not swinging. Maybe she went back into the house. *God, please, don't let me have fucked up.*

He rounded the corner.

The swing was empty. Cindy was nowhere in sight.

From the news reports, Paul knew that time was crucial in solving missing person cases; minutes counted. After a quick sweep of the backyard and the house, he called 9-1-1. After imparting enough information for the operator to dispatch the police, he told her he was going back outside to search for his daughter. The woman implored him to stay on the line, but he placed his cell phone on the table—he had no time to listen to her pleas—and ran through the front door.

If Cindy was taken, the kidnapper's most probable means of escape was through the woods at the back of the property, but Paul checked the street first. It would take precious seconds but would alleviate any doubt he would have later if he didn't find her out back. Flying down the concrete steps, he ran to the sidewalk and looked up and down the street. No vehicles were in motion. No stranger ran along the blacktop with his daughter in tow. He checked one last time before sprinting to the backyard.

As Paul reached the swing set, sirens perforated the silence. The sound had not slowed him. He charged past the swing set into the woods, looking for Cindy or any clues she had struggled or been dragged through the scrub and old oaks. Even if she was carried, he knew Cindy would have put up a fight, as she'd been taught to do. He had reviewed the instructions with her every evening in light of the missing children. The lessons had scared her at first, but he had stressed their importance. For reassurance, he had promised it would never happen to her. Over the previous three weeks, the "what to do if a stranger approaches you" lesson had morphed into a routine part of her bedtime ritual. In an exasperated monotone, Cindy would always pre-empt his questions with a smile and say it was important to always be prepared. What he could not teach her, what he could not prepare her for was the unthinkable—that she might not have the ability to resist. Muscle, chemical agents, or unspeakable violence might overpower her...or something worse.

If Cindy were still alive—*she had to be*—would she think him a liar now, his promises empty? He had fucked up, and in the worst way. If they found her—*no, not if, when*—she would likely never trust him again.

He scrambled through the woods, searching for scraps of clothing, a fresh path, footprints—anything. The thought never occurred to him that he might be destroying evidence. Pushing farther into the woods, he paused and screamed her name. He prayed for an answer, even if it was a strained call for help. All he wanted was to hear her voice again. Shoving brush aside and trampling over long, unkempt grass, he frantically swept the area, searching for any sign of her.

He heard the swish of branches behind him. A male voice pleaded, "Please stop. Let us handle this." He ignored it and continued on.

He stopped when a small red object came into view clinging to a high-hanging branch.

"Stay where you are, sir, don't move!"

A cop, his pistol drawn and aimed, stood crouched twenty feet away. Ignoring the officer, he stayed focused on the red object. Heedless of additional warnings, he paced slowly toward it and grabbed hold. It was one of Cindy's barrettes. The one she had worn this morning. His throat constricted and tears fell.

"Sir, is your name 'Lane'?"

He turned to face the officer. Handing him the red barrette, he mumbled, "...my daughter's."

The officer gently placed a hand on Paul's shoulder and led him back to the house. The questioning began. They asked him the same things over and over again, sometimes in different ways, which only made him even more frustrated. He realized his replies were lame, vague. He was giving them nothing to work with. His answers reinforced his guilt of leaving her alone, and the questioner's clinical responses did nothing to dissuade him of it. When finished, they told him to remain where he was as the searchers combed the woods. Instead, he sat on the front step, trying not to think the worst.

Flashing blue lights reflected in the windows of neighboring homes. Police lined both sides of the street along the length of Paul's front yard, the officers standing abreast, keeping onlookers from trespassing onto the property—onto a crime scene. A news crew milled about nearby; all the spectators except for the officers had their heads turned toward his home.

As an engineer, Paul was hard-wired to study the downside of a situation, to assume the worst. From the moment he'd seen the first report of a missing child, he had started planning preventative measures. He followed the news daily, his concern rising with each missing child. *How could they disappear so easily?* This line of questioning inevitably led to a more disturbing thought—*how did the parents of those children cope with their loss?* He never failed to shudder when the footage of a mom or dad flashed on the screen imploring for the return of their child. He found himself close to tears imagining anything that god-awful ever happening to Cindy.

Allowed across the police barrier, a young African-American woman was headed in his direction

"Mr. Lane?"

"Yes."

"I'm Lynne, the mother of Lisa Carole, one of the missing children."

Paul nodded. "I recognize you."

"I know what you are going through, so I know this is a difficult time to talk. But I wanted you to know you're not alone. Lisa has been gone for a month now, and I won't give up searching for her. I rushed down here when I heard on the police scanner what happened. I'm praying Cindy's disappearance is not linked to any of the others, but if it is, I want to be here if they gather any clues. If they come across anything that can help me find my Lisa."

Despite his own grief, Paul felt badly for the woman. He wondered how she spent her days now. Did she sit at home listening to the police scanner? How much time did she spend at the police station or calling the FBI for updates?

They shook hands. "Do you mind if I sit here with you?" she asked.

He did mind. He wanted to be alone. His mind fogged with regret and worry, his gut so hollow he felt weightless, company was the last thing he needed. To crawl inside himself and turn numb was his refuge from the consequences of his neglect. The only person he wanted by his side...the only person he wanted to talk to was his daughter. Only, he saw so much anguish in the woman's eyes. Though she was here in the hope of gleaning information about her own daughter, there was little hope in those eyes. He imagined his were as bleak as hers.

"Yes. Please, sit." He made room on the step.

Together they sat waiting for the results of the search.

FOUR

As usual, Manuel woke at 6:00 a.m., showered, dressed, and made his way to the Goffstown Diner. Having been a regular for the past fifteen years, the waitresses would escort him to *his* table. He preferred to sit in the back room away from other diners, where he could spread out the daily newspaper, enjoy his coffee, and eat breakfast at his leisure. However, today was Saturday; his customary reservation did not apply on weekends. Because the restaurant was close to full, the only table available was by the windows along the front of the building.

Despite his mild annoyance, he smiled when Sandi, the young server—his favorite—approached.

"Good morning, Mr. Chance!" The loose hairs that stuck out of her ponytail indicated a harried morning. She puffed the bangs out of her eyes. "I managed to save you a seat. It's by the window. Sorry, but it's the best I could do."

"That's fine, Sandi. Thank you."

She led him to the table. "The usual?"

"Yes, please." Manuel opened the paper and sat back in his chair. The bold headline had him sitting bolt upright.

GOFFSTOWN GIRL MISSING

Duck Lady's image flashed before his eyes.

Mrs. Delaney had not followed up with her request for him to visit her home. Two weeks had passed since their conversation, and despite his initial apprehension, Manuel was disappointed not to have heard from her, so he had decided to forget about the woman and her offer. She was obviously mentally impaired from her ordeal, the tie between her husband and the missing children a psychotic invention. As he read the article, he wondered if this latest case would stoke her delusions.

"Excuse me."

Manuel jumped at the intrusion.

It was Sandi with a glass pot in her hand. "Sorry, I didn't mean to startle you. I brought some coffee. Your order will be up in a few minutes."

He blushed. "Oh, no problem. I was reading the front page," he lightly shook the paper to make his point, "and I was lost in thought."

"Yeah," sighed Sandi. "I heard about it this morning when I came in. This makes five, I think. The first from Goffstown, though. I can't imagine what those parents are going through. Seems nowhere is safe anymore." She poured the coffee.

"Yeah, I know," he said. "Thanks."

"Be back in a few minutes."

Manuel returned to the paper.

The article didn't have many details beyond stating that the girl had vanished the day before, but the identity of her father took Manuel by surprise. Paul Lane. Although he was acquainted with Paul, he wouldn't consider him a friend. When Paul had worked on architectural projects in Goffstown over the years, Manuel had interviewed him three or four times. He was a nice guy, and Manuel felt sorry for him.

As he ate his second egg, a movement outside the window caught his eye. Manuel stopped chewing. It was Delaney. Indecision struck him. Was her offer still good? Had she heard about the missing Goffstown girl? If she were crazy, he might be opening a can of worms and wasting his time. Though her pace was slower than a pensioner traveling through a crosswalk, he needed to decide—and soon.

As he glanced down at the paper, the face of the missing girl peered up at him. This was not some anonymous child in a neighboring town. It was Paul's daughter. If Manuel were to follow up with Delaney and her suspicions were correct, he might be able to help the child. Not to mention get the scoop of his life.

He fished out a twenty-dollar bill from his wallet and threw it on the table. Leaving the restaurant, he caught up to Duck Lady after she was a block past the diner and called out to her. She stopped but did not turn around. Manuel stepped in front, blocking her.

"Mrs. Delaney, I expected you to contact me the day after we met at my office."

When he had first met the woman, her eyes were half-closed, dull. Now, as she stared at him, he could see a spark. Eyes fully open, her withering glare was penetrating; he felt like a scolded, petulant child silently put into place. The woman's gaze shifted to his chest. When she looked up, all trace of her steely demeanor had vanished. With lids drooped, her face softened.

"Mr. Chance. I was on my way to your office." She stepped closer to him. "Yes. The timing wasn't right. My husband fell ill and missed a few days of work. While I was administering to him, he appeared so fragile, much like he was after my god-forsaken experience. I thought I was wrong about him, and I was embarrassed. Once he recovered, things were fine for a few days, and I all but dismissed our conversation in your office. Two days ago, he reverted to his sullen ways and withdrew. When I heard about the latest incident, my fears returned. I need to know, Mr. Chance, if the disappearance of that little girl yesterday has anything to do with him."

The sincerity in her tone gave her explanation weight.

"So, what do you want me to do?" asked Manuel.

"Donald is at work today, trying to make up the hours he lost. He works until five o'clock, but sometimes he comes home for lunch around noon. Come over at one-thirty. That will give you at least a couple of hours to check out the house and the barn before he comes home."

"The barn?"

She nodded. "Yes, I want you to check his study, the basement, and the barn."

"Have you checked those places out?"

"Only the study. I can navigate the stairs to the basement, but it's difficult, and he keeps the barn locked."

"How will I get into the barn?"

"Through a window in the back. He cracks it open for ventilation."

"Mrs. Delaney, are you sure your husband won't come home early?"

"Yes. We need the money."

"Okay. Let's suppose I do find something that points to his involvement. If so, I will have to alert the authorities right away."

The woman tightened her face and then regained her composure.

"Yes, Mr. Chance, I agree. I only ask that you show me what you find. Then, you may go to the police with the evidence. Bring it with you and present it to them."

"And you will tell me your story?"

"I told you I would."

Manuel offered his hand to shake. She ignored it. Instead, she reached into her dress pocket and handed him a piece of paper. "My address. I will expect you at one-thirty this afternoon, Mr. Chance."

"I'll be there."

Without acknowledging the reply, Mrs. Delaney turned and duck-walked back in the direction from which she had come.

FIVE

Cindy blinked in confusion. *I must have been taking a nap.* An odor, like the chemicals used in her dad's basement, made her sniffle. It wasn't strong, but it wouldn't go away. *Did I spill something on my dress?*

Her back ached. It was on something hard. Wherever she was, it wasn't her bed or the couch. She forced her eyes open as wide as she could, but they wanted to close right back up, and rubbing them didn't take the sleepiness away.

"Daddy?" No answer. "Daddy? Daddy?"

Straining to keep her eyes open in the gloom she looked up to see wooden boards high above. Even in this light, they looked dirty.

Where am I? I want my daddy!

Sobs racked her body. She turned onto her side, pulled her knees closer to her chest, and screamed for her daddy until her throat was hoarse. Moments later, exhausted, she whimpered until the tears stopped flowing.

He can't hear me, that's why he hasn't come. I have to find him.

What light there was came from a single window, though a curtain prevented her from seeing through it. The walls, like the ceiling, were all wooden boards. There was no furniture, but she could make out a heavy door at the far end of the room; streaks of light shone through the gaps around it.

She got up. There was a rattle-like noise, and she felt a tugging on one of her feet. She looked down and saw something wrapped around her left ankle. *How did that get there?* It wasn't tight enough to hurt, but she didn't like it. Not sure what it was, she shook her foot as she walked toward the door, but she didn't make it far. Something pulled at her left leg. A chain, like the one on her swing set, was hooked onto the object clamped over her ankle. Following it with her eyes, she saw the other end fastened to the wall.

I'm tied up like Mr. White's dog!

She shuddered, and tears rolled down her cheeks. Was she a pet, now? Would she have to eat out of a bowl? She didn't want to poop and pee outside.

"Daddy, where are you?" Covering her face with her hands, she whispered, "Come get me. Come get me. Come get me. Come get—"

A sound at the front of the room quieted her.

The door was opening.

"Daddy?"

Forgetting about the chain, she rushed ahead, coming to a whip-snap stop when the bound leg gave out from under her. The floor rushed toward her, her forehead absorbing the brunt of the fall. Stunned, she lay there for a few seconds. When the pain kicked in, her agonized cries were pleading and mournful.

She peed.

"Daddy," she pleaded softly, "where are you?"

The sound of approaching footsteps reached her ears.

Daddy?

She lifted her head.

In the dim light, she could see a man approaching, and the silhouettes of four kids behind him. Older than her daddy, the man had a smile on his face. But something was wrong. His eyes didn't look right. Half-closed and focused intensely on hers, she felt as if he were looking inside her.

The four kids—two girls and two boys—wore blank expressions, their eyes wide open, staring, scaring her more than the man did. While the four of them stopped a few feet from her, the man walked up to her. He got so close she could only see his legs. She lifted her head higher to see his face.

He bent down until his head was slightly above hers. "What's your name, young girl?"

"I—I want my daddy."

"Who should I tell him is asking?"

"C—Cindy."

The man ran his fingers across her forehead. When he pulled them back, they were bloody.

"You saved me some trouble, Cindy. I won't have to cut you."

Her eyes widened.

"I need you to take off your dress."

Words of warning from her daddy came to her. *No! That's not good!*

The man snapped his fingers and one of the girls moved beside him, holding a bathrobe.

"I'm not going to ask you again, Cindy. Take off your dress and put this on. We will turn around while you change."

Trembling, Cindy took the robe and held it against her chest. The man and the children turned their backs.

After undressing and slipping on the robe, Cindy announced, "I'm done." Her voice was low, weak.

The group turned and faced her again.

Cindy held out the dress.

"Thank you," said the man, who used it to wipe the blood off her forehead. He removed a key from his pocket and unlocked the chain from her ankle. "Now, I want you to come with us." Motioning to the girl behind him, he added, "Lisa, please take her hand and follow me."

Lisa led Cindy through a door to a much bigger, brighter room. Lit candles were scattered along the floor and walls. She noticed cots all lined up in a circle, surrounding a huge, empty table. Above it, hanging from the ceiling, was a cross—just like the ones she had seen in church. Only there was no man on this cross. And it was upside down.

Thank God, this is almost over. The man leaned forward and placed a hand on the girl's head.

"Cindy, I am going to take you home soon," he explained, "but first you need to meet someone very special."

The young girl burst into tears. "I don't want to meet anyone. I want to go home right now. I want my daddy."

"This will be over soon. I'm going to ask you to lie down on one of these cots. You'll fall asleep quickly. It will be like taking a nap. When you wake up, you will be with your father."

"I don't want to take a nap, I want my daddy, now!"

He took a deep breath, controlling his anger. Bending low, he brought his face close to hers. "I'm not going to tell you again. Lie down on that bed, NOW."

Cringing, Cindy backed away. She looked toward him, then to the cot. Her head shook a silent *no.* She turned to the children standing next to him. They all offered nods of encouragement. She wiped her eyes and stepped to the cot. It was low to the ground and she climbed on without assistance. Whimpering, she lay back on the mattress.

He wrapped leather restraints over her hands and ankles, drawing them in tight.

"Okay. I need each of you to do the same."

Without comment, the kids complied.

He secured them as he had Cindy.

He had been preparing for months for this day, spending all his free time with the kids after he'd taken them. His wife's incantations kept them calm. Nighttime cold medicine also proved useful. Some children had been more resistant than others, but after weeks of solitude, light deprivation, restraint, and unrelenting indoctrination, they all obeyed, listening to him without question or fear. Except for Cindy, the fifth member needed for the ritual, whose presence was unnerving as it was unexpected.

The previous night, his wife had roused him from sleep, insisting he conduct the ceremony this evening, weeks ahead of schedule. He had protested, explaining that he'd yet made final plans for stealing another kid. Her glare was all the response he needed. Leaping out of bed, he had considered his options. There were only two. The first was a young boy he spotted every morning walking toward his bus stop. The problem would be that the boy was alone only for the span of a block before he joined others at the bus stop. He would have to hide between houses to grab the kid, and the chances of detection were too high. While staking out the boy, he had discovered Cindy, noting that she was occasionally left alone in the backyard. Her house backed onto woodland, and some exploratory driving around revealed a road behind the woods he could use for access. He would have to pull over and park in the dirt, leaving tread marks, but he had planned for that. Luck had been on his side this morning when he crouched in the scrub and saw her on the swing.

Months of his wife's research and planning were coming to fruition.

Cindy pulled at the restraints. The man had told her she would be taking a nap, but she was far from sleepy, though she was weak. All the screaming, crying, and resistance she had put up was taking a toll on her. Tired muscles and a sore throat wore down her resolve, and she lay back to rest.

The man sat on the cot at the center on the circle, flipping through the pages of a book. He stopped to read for a few moments.

"Okay, kids, you ready? As I promised, you are going to meet someone wonderful."

There was no response.

"All right, I'm going to read something. You won't understand the words, but I want you to listen carefully. You'll feel sleepy, but don't worry, it won't last long. Here we go."

He was right; Cindy didn't understand a word he said. It sounded like something from one of the Spanish television channels. His voice was calm, soothing, and she was lulled by his hushed tones. Though the words were foreign to her, they somehow conjured images of shadows, dark and wavering, filling the room. They were standing tall, but crooked. She blinked, unable to understand what she was seeing. A weight settled in her head and she closed her eyes. When she reopened them, the shadows had form. They were trees, only they didn't look right. Their trunks were missing bark—in its place hung ugly tangles of spindly knots. A black, greasy smoke hovered at the base of the trunks. The trees were bare, their branches and tops gone, as if they had been ripped off. She'd seen a tree just like this once on a trip to the park; *struck by lightning*, her father said. *Could lightning have hit every one of these trees?*

She fought against the growing weight in her head. Losing the battle, her eyes closed again and blackness began to claim her. A floating sensation followed. Afraid of falling, she willed herself to open her eyes.

She found herself looking down at a young girl lying on a cot. She gasped, cried out, but heard no sound. Panicking, she screamed for help, the continuing silence feeding her fear.

"Daddy! Daddy, help me, I don't want to be here!"

She looked around in the hope someone else was there, even if it was the man who had brought her here. She saw only darkness. *What happened to the trees? They're gone.*

In an instant, they reappeared.

The black smoke had risen. It had floated higher, past their damaged tips, and it was still in motion. A breeze pushed at the smoke, rotating it, whipping the black fog into a swirling frenzy.

I've seen this before. In a movie.

Cindy made the connection. Her mind froze when she recognized what she was looking at. A tornado.

The tornado from *The Wizard of Oz*.

I don't want to be sucked up into that. I don't want to meet the Wicked Witch.

Only, she had no control. There was no body to move, no eyes to close. She was just *there*.

In the center of the twisting black smoke, a dim light appeared. Against that backdrop, a shape formed. It was round, dark, and denser than the smoke that encircled it. Instead of fearing the sight, an odd mixture of calm and curiosity overcame her. *Is that the Wizard?*

Facial features came into focus. Cindy knew right away it wasn't the Wizard. This face wasn't round or pink and there was no joy in its eyes. Instead, it stretched long and thin from its hairline to its chin. It had no bushy mustache that stuck out past rosy cheeks, no birds' nests for eyebrows. This face was clean-shaven and as black and wrinkled as the cover on her father's bible. As Cindy stared, she found herself drifting toward its egg-shaped, yellow eyes. A part of her knew she should be scared, that she should look away. That part of her slipped away as her curiosity grew along with her awe.

Though she was too young to fully grasp the concept of theology, she accepted God's existence without question. After all, everyone else did. Schoolmates, teachers, relatives—all had invoked His name, and she came to understand the idea of an afterlife, and a being who watched over everybody. As Cindy gazed at the face, she wondered if she had died and gone to heaven. *Was this God?*

"Children, you are my vessel."

The words slammed into Cindy, the voice loud, gruff, without warmth. It said *children*. She could not see anyone else. Was it talking about the other kids on the cots? Were they with her? Behind or out of sight? Were they all invisible angels?

"I am joining with you. Together, we will make a new home, a better home. We will be worshipped."

She had another brief moment of unease, but before long, acceptance overwhelmed her. She wanted a new home, a better home. Though she wasn't sure what it would be like to be worshipped, an image of people serving her every request came to her. All of this would make the man-face happy, and nothing was more important right now. She would do anything to please him.

"Not all of you will return. Those who stay will provide me with nourishment—your innocence is potent. The pain you will suffer sustains me."

The yellow eyes blazed.

Desire fueled Cindy.

Her thoughts blurred.

Then, as the man-face had said, there was pain.

A sensation of tumbling, speeding through the air, overwhelmed her. When Cindy's essence crashed back onto the cot, it had company.

SIX

Long and sprawling, Mountain Road led up and over the north peak of the two Uncanoonuc Mountains. Their name originated from the Algonquian people; translated into English it meant *woman's breasts*. The north mountain's base commenced at one end of Goffstown's Main Street. With its granite cliffs, pine and oak trees sloping away from downtown, it provided a serene setting, especially in the fall when the red, green, and yellow autumn leaves blazed. Add in the lake that ran through the center of town, the concrete bridge that traversed it, and the old-fashioned popcorn stand at the other end of Main Street, Goffstown was the quintessential, quaint New England town. It had more than earned its way onto the specialty postcard racks at general stores around the state.

Appearances aside, Goffstown was far from perfect.

Blood tainted the town's history.

As Manuel navigated the twists and turns of Mountain Road, he recalled some of the tragedies his newspaper had published: the convenience store robbery turned deadly, the hit-and-run at the high school, a husband shooting his schoolteacher wife to death, the mother who drowned her children, and the Moore House serial killer. All these stories came to him quickly. Too quickly. If he were superstitious, he would check *yes* in the "Is your town cursed?" column when given a quiz. But he was a practical man, understanding that small-town living brought unique problems—problems that could test a person's sanity.

Like bread that had spent too long in the back of the refrigerator, staleness had overtaken his community. Elected under the ruse of continuity and preservation—when laziness or apathy was more likely the reasons—the same politicians remained in office. The more gifted young people had moved out of town, absconding with their creativity, abandoning the ennui of their lives. Annoyances and grudges festered, often with disastrous results. In Manuel's opinion, Goffstown reveled in its past, content to idle and age while the rest of the world moved forward. From the horror movies he had seen and the scary books he had read, he supposed that if an evil curse had been placed on the town, it *could* be lifted. Indifference, however, would prove it impossible to exorcise.

Turning hard on an incline, Manuel spotted a clearing ahead. He stopped to read a street number on the mailbox. He had found Mrs. Delaney's home. He turned into the gravel driveway, drove the length of a football field, rounded a bend, and arrived at a Cape Cod-style house. He stepped from his car and leaned against the front fender.

The house was small, unassuming, clad with deep brown wooden shiplap boards. It had weathered well; he saw no fading or cracks in the wood. The roof appeared solid, without sags, and its black shingles looked new. A sturdy porch with a pair of rocking chairs stretched along the front of the house, giving the dwelling a homey feel. It was a typical middle-class home for the area, no doubt a twin to many others on the mountain.

The barn sat a couple hundred feet to the right of the house. A dark red gambrel, it stood almost three stories high, but lacked the upkeep of the residence; knots had bled through the paint, turning the wall into a mosaic of distorted faces and creatures. Such barns had been popular back in the day for farms that stored hay and housed cattle, but Manuel saw no indication of livestock in the area. He assumed it functioned now as storage or as a work area for Mr. Delaney. The question was, what was the man working at? Worse, what was he storing? Manuel thought of the missing children and shuddered. *I can't believe I'm doing this.*

"Mr. Chance."

Mrs. Delaney called from the front porch, waving him over. Approaching her, he noticed a not-so-subtle transformation in her appearance since their conversation earlier that morning. She had ditched the black dress, replacing it with a white one, again from neck to ankle. While the dress flowed freely from her hips, it was snug on top. She had brushed her hair. Wavy and full-bodied, it draped over her shoulders and rested on her chest. Positioned as it was, she could have been a model in a shampoo commercial. As he reached the steps to the porch, Manuel noted she wasn't wearing shoes. Her feet were delicate, feminine—quite unexpected for someone who hobbled when she walked. Gazing upward to her face, he was not surprised to find her frowning. What did surprise him was the trace of maroon lipstick gracing her lips.

Her eyes were softer than he remembered. The application of purple eyeliner diminished the harsh coolness of her ashen pupils. Her cheeks were fuller now, tinted with a light shade of pink. A pleasant odor assailed his nose. *Perfume.* For the first time, Manuel found the woman attractive. He had to admit she possessed a tangible beauty, but the unfortunate curvature of her back and its resulting complications precluded any comparison to a Ms. New Hampshire.

Manuel was aware his appreciation of the woman had come too swiftly. Manipulation came to mind. Had she fixed herself up for him? Was this meeting a pretense for seduction? If so, for what purpose? The answer came quickly.

Mrs. Delaney cleared her throat. "Mr. Chance, I have an appointment I must attend to at four o'clock. It's important, and, as you might have noticed, I am preparing for it. This gives us at least two hours, plenty of time for you to inspect the premises. I would like you to start with his den. I have been through it and didn't find anything, but I would like you to double-check."

Manuel nodded.

"Then, I'd like you to inspect the basement. There is a light switch on the wall to your left as you go down the stairs. I doubt you will find anything there either. I don't use those stairs often, but I am home most of the time my husband is, and I have not or seen or heard anything that leads me to believe he has anything down there. But I want to be sure."

"Okay."

"After that, I'd like you to check out the barn. The window is open a few inches so you can lift it and crawl through. I've left a flashlight there for you. There are switches by the barn doors to light up the main portion of the barn and the loft. If you have trouble getting through the window, there is a stepladder leaning against the wall. To be honest, if my husband is involved with any of these disappearances, I think the evidence will be in the barn."

Manuel leaned toward the woman. "And if I find evidence?"

He could smell her perfume. The scent and her proximity had a curious effect on him.

"Mr. Chance...."

"Please, call me Manny."

She stared into his eyes. "Manny...I told you that if you find evidence my husband was involved with these crimes, you may involve the police. I stand by my words. I will also sit for the interview you requested, whether you find something or not."

Manuel wanted to break away from her stare, but an urge to pull her violently toward him took root. He saw himself reaching his arm up, placing an open hand against the back of her head. Her mouth would part, but her features would be a mask of confusion. He shivered at an impulse to force his lips against hers. Visions played before his eyes of Ms. Delaney resisting in his arms as he caressed her breasts. He imagined his passion intense enough, flattering enough, to overcome any reluctance. Soon, he knew, her soft hesitating sighs would become moans. Intoxicated by the fantasy, he stepped closer to her, pausing only when his nose was inches from hers. A scent, raw, more intense than her perfume, overpowered him. The consequences of his arousal made itself known. While she hadn't smiled, she wasn't frowning, either.

"Manny...you need to start looking."

Standing alone at the rear of the barn, Manuel leaned against the wall and lowered his head. *What happened back there?*

Ms. Delaney was present when he searched the den. Hovering at the doorway, she observed his every move, offering no comment as he went through desk drawers, bookshelves, and a closet. Finding nothing, he shrugged and waited for further instructions. She gestured toward a door in the hallway between the kitchen and the den. He nodded and followed her to the door. She opened it, flicked a switch, and a descending staircase lit up.

48

"I can't easily walk down these stairs, but I'll be here at the top," she said. "It's wide open down there, one big room. When you search, check around and behind the furnace. We heat with oil, not wood, so it's not as though he could have burned anything in it. While he keeps most of his tools in the barn, he does have a worktable down there. Pull out any boxes he may have stored beneath it."

Manuel studied the woman's face. Her wrinkles sunk deep, mapping pasty white flesh. How could he have lusted after her?

"Anything else I should look for?"

"I'm pretty sure if there is anything to find, it would be in the barn, so don't spend too much time down there. We have over an hour before I have to leave, and most of that time should be spent over there."

As he pushed past her and started down the stairs, she reached out and patted his shoulder. He stopped for an instant. The touch sent warm tremors all the way down to his groin.

"Go, Manny. We don't have much time."

Though part of him was disappointed, he obeyed. The look around the basement took under ten minutes, and he found no evidence of misdeeds. He had to admit the search was half-assed, partly due to his confused feelings. It had been some time since he had had sex, but still, there were plenty of reasons to run as far away as he could. For one, she was married, and he had learned long ago to stay away from that temptation. And, though he never considered himself shallow, Ms. Delaney's looks and appearance were far from appealing. Not that he was a young buck, but she resembled a grandmother with osteoporosis. Why in the hell did he get so damn horny when he was close to her?

When he was back upstairs, he waved and shook his head *no*. "Thank you, Manny, for doing this," she said, as she showed him to the front door. "I—I'm feeling better about everything already. If you don't find anything in the barn, I will be very relieved." She reached out and held his hand. "And very grateful."

A charge, like low-wattage electricity, traveled up his arms. He pulled his hands back and walked to the barn with his head spinning.

As he leaned against the wall with one hand, he used the other to unzip his fly. He masturbated to mental images of her naked, sitting on top of him, giving him the ride of his life. He ejaculated on the wall, and only then did his head clear and the tension release from his body. Ignoring the dripping mess, he zipped his fly back up and positioned the stepladder under the sole window in the wall. He climbed through and entered the barn.

There was insufficient light for a thorough search. Finding the light switch, fluorescent bulbs cast a cool white brilliance inside the barn. He went to work.

Starting on ground level, he inspected three workbenches against the walls of the barn, and an additional bench in the middle of the area. He was pleased to find that her husband was a meticulous man who had a place for everything, and everything was in its place. There was little clutter on the benches, or anywhere else in the spacious barn. He kept an eye out for children's toys, clothing, and bloodstains, but found nothing. Four tires and a jack were neatly stacked against the wall. He noticed slight wear on the treads, but enough remained for at least another summer season. The hand tools were worn but clean, as were the power tools— hard to believe the barn served as a workshop. Maybe Donald told his wife it was so he could get away from her. Satisfied there was no evidence on the ground floor, Manuel made his way to a set of wooden steps that led to the loft. At the top of the staircase, he stopped and gazed. The loft was empty. There was a layer of dust on the wooden floor, but no footprints.

He had seen enough.

After turning the lights off, he crawled back out the way he had come, closed the window, and placed the stepladder back where he had found it. He couldn't have been more pleased. If he had found something, who knew how the police would have handled his involvement. Worse, who knew how it might have affected Ms. Delaney. Now she could give him her story without this fear hanging over her head. He had all but forgotten the erotic impulses that had come over him in her presence; instead, he focused on how to set up the interviews. When he turned the corner to the barn, she was waiting for him in the doorway of the house.

"Ms. Delaney, I have good news. I found nothing out of the ordinary in the barn."

She responded with a grin. "Thank you, Manny. You put my mind to rest."

Her tongue slipped out from her mouth and she licked her upper lip.

I wonder what else that tongue can lick.

The thought caught him off guard. Why was he thinking this way? Was she coming on to him? Even if she was, why was he responding? He had to admit, she looked good in that dress. The impulse to flirt with her was strong, but he resolved to stick with the business at hand.

"Now that the search is over," he said, "can we discuss the interview you promised me?"

"Yes, of course." She took his hand. "Come inside. I am so grateful for what you have done."

Her touch sent waves of pleasure through him. Her hand was small, fitting comfortably inside his. It was also warm, and his fingers wrapped gently around it. Somewhere in his mind, there was an awareness that his sexual desire increased when she was in close proximity, but the thought was elusive, slipping away as soon as he focused on it.

She led him to the kitchen table, which was set with plates, water glasses, silverware, napkins, and coffee mugs. She pulled out one of the chairs.

"Please, Manny, sit."

Ms. Delaney released her handhold. She stood close to him, their knees touching. Gazing down, her grin grew wider. "Manny, I want to show you how grateful I am."

His heart beat faster.

Reaching around, she removed one of the glasses from the table. She kneeled before him and placed the glass on the floor. She cupped her breasts.

"You like these, Manny?"

He nodded.

The woman reached out to his groin, pulling down the zipper. She parted the opening, moved aside the split in his underwear, and grasped his penis. With a tug, she exposed it. Leaning forward, her mouth enveloped him.

Manuel watched her head raise and lower, again and again. He held tightly onto the seat of the chair with both hands, thrusting his hips to her rhythm. If it weren't for having masturbated earlier, he would have exploded the second she grabbed his cock, but even so, he knew he wouldn't last long. Groaning, he raised his head to the ceiling and closed his eyes. He was steel in her mouth. Her tongue felt so good, so warm, so soft. Her fingers cradled his balls, and his back arched. When her teeth scraped against him, the pressure was too much. He exploded in her mouth. As his semen pumped, the combined odor of chlorine and musk drifted up to his nose. He wrapped his hands around her head and pushed her down, forcing himself deeper inside her mouth. When it was over, when the last drop had eased out, he opened his eyes, slid his hips forward, and sunk into the chair.

Mrs. Delaney reached for the water glass. Bringing it to her lips, she let the semen flow from her mouth into the receptacle. Instead of spitting, she let it drip until the flow stopped. She stood, placed the cup on the table, and used a cloth napkin to wipe the remains from her lips. When finished, she tossed the napkin onto the floor.

"Mr. Chance, please zip yourself back up and leave now. I will be late for my appointment."

What in the hell just happened? Manuel's hands shook as he pulled out from the driveway. Did he really get a blowjob from an unattractive, married, hunchbacked woman who'd dismissed him the moment he'd finished? And what was with her spitting his semen into a glass? She placed it next to her before she started, so why not just pull away if she didn't care for the taste? He was disgusted with himself. I *should go for a long drive to think this through.*

After he had zipped himself up, he had spoken her name, his voice just above a whisper, to prompt a response from her. Emptiness had overcome him; he needed to assuage his guilt with discussion. Not only did Ms. Delaney remain silent, she refused to make eye contact. After wiping her lips on the napkin, she motioned to the front door and asked him to leave.

She hadn't escorted him out. Her only comment came as he stepped onto the porch, his car keys in hand. With her head lowered, she said something along the lines of "We'll talk later." It wasn't as if he expected pillow talk, but damn, this didn't feel right. She had seduced *him,* so he didn't think an apology was in order, but should he have thanked her? Was a goodbye kiss called for? He appraised the woman. Despite her fancy clothing, he thought her unappealing, ugly. That sexy, mature woman who had seduced him morphed back to the cold, physically fragile Duck Lady he had been dealing with.

He spent the rest of the ride chiding himself for becoming sexually involved with her.

Driving aimlessly did nothing to put the affair into order. It was time to go home. Maybe after a drink—or two—it might make some sense to him. Pulling up to his house, his jaw dropped. Police cruisers with their blue lights flashing lined both sides of the street, bracketing his home. Two more had parked in his driveway. He slowed to find a place to park and jumped when an officer stepped out in front of his car. Manuel faced a drawn handgun, aimed at his windshield. Shouts for him to stop and get out of the car with his hands up came from all directions. He whipped his head from left to right to see who was shouting. More officers, crouched in a shooting stance, surrounded him. After breaking, he put the car in "Park".

He recognized the officer in front of his car as Captain Bechtel. "Mr. Chance," the officer called, "please come out of your vehicle with both your hands held up where we can see them."

More a gesture of disbelief than refusal, Manuel shook his head.

"DO IT NOW!"

Jolted, Manuel opened the door and raised his hands high. "Hey," he asked the closest officer, "what's all this about?" The cop grabbed him by the shoulders and spun him around. Shoved against the car with his face pressed against the window, the officer jerked Manuel's hands behind him and snapped a pair of handcuffs over his wrists. The cuffs pressed deep into his flesh and he grimaced. A blow to his lower back had him howling as his knees buckled. His gun holstered, Captain Bechtel stood off to Manuel's side. Manuel pleaded, "Please, tell me, what the hell is going on?"

"Are you Manuel Chance?"

"Yes. You know I am. I've interviewed you a number of times for the paper."

"You are hereby arrested on the suspicion of kidnapping."

Manuel's mouth dropped. "Kidnapping? Whose kidnapping?"

The captain's eyes burned with fury. "Jennifer Bailey, Timothy Sullivan, and Adam Sharpe."

Manuel froze. Those were the names of three of the missing children.

SEVEN

Ms. Delaney's fingertips glided over her scarred, wrinkled skin-canvas. Ink-blackened symbols and silhouettes reacted to her touch—quivering, merging, dividing—supplicants of her desire. Dark as coal, her nipples rose from the stimulation. Though painful, her back arched as she sighed. Physical pleasure was not her only goal. The Dark Master fed on the release of her euphoric energy during masturbation, and the simple thought of pleasing him proved to be as erotic as any self-induced orgasm.

Neither Mrs. Delaney's tryst with Mr. Chance nor her subsequent journey into town after he had left played any part in her lust. Her carnal yearning had everything to do with the ceremony her husband was performing in the old ice cellar in a shed behind the barn. The broken body she inhabited was in no condition to descend to the ancient bunker to participate in the ritual. Because of what she had come to call her *sacrifice* at the hands of her four abductors, she had missed many opportunities to join her husband in their preparations. Though physically bereft, she was determined to play a contributing part in the ritual.

She caressed a sigil at the back of her right knee. Focusing her thoughts, she queried the Dark Master on how she could assist her husband. The answer came quickly. She was to call the Dark Master out. She did, and he was there. He was on top of her, inside her, overflowing her cavity with ebony seed. He would impregnate her—not with a child, he said, but with more power than she had already been granted. When he withdrew, streams of black semen dripped onto her ass and over her thighs, forming puddles on the sheet. Before he vanished, he commanded her to spread his offering over her body, to use her sense of smell and breathe him in, and to swallow his gift to nourish her. She was to remain fouled and wait for her husband's return.

"What happened to you?" An oily black substance covered his wife, soaking into the sheet beneath her. *Did her tattoos melt?* He discounted the notion. Her skin was still dark—no pink that he could see. Where she was free of ink—her hands, feet, face—she glistened with the gross stuff.

"I assisted you in the ceremony. The Dark Master came to me."

His shoulders stiffened. "What the... is that stuff jizz? It's bad enough you had to give a blowjob to that newspaper guy, now you're letting a demon fuck you?"

Her eyes narrowed. "Are you questioning me?"

Did he see a flash of red in them? He took a step back, averting his gaze. "No. I-I'm sorry."

His wife's response was quick and firm. "Know your place." She paused before speaking again. "Tell me, what happened?"

"I carried out the ritual, speaking the words you gave me." He resumed eye contact. "Nothing happened at first. After a few minutes, the room got hot, the air was so dry my throat and nose hurt from breathing. I took my eyes off the kids to look around, and when I turned back to them, they were all asleep. Well, they had their eyes closed, anyway. They were stiff as hell, turning blue, like they were frozen in place. I touched one of them, and my fingers burned when I touched his throat..."

"YOU WEREN'T SUPPOSED TO TOUCH THEM!"

He grimaced from the fury of her outburst. "I know, I know." A quiver in his voice betrayed his fear. "I thought I screwed something up. Maybe said the words wrong. They all looked dead. I was scared, so I checked for a pulse."

The woman's face went slack, and her jaw dropped. "Were they all dead? Did you fuck it up?"

"No, not the boy I checked." He sighed, and added, "Not then, at least."

"Cut the description shit out, get to the end, how many survived?"

"Two. Two of the girls made it back."

A smile dressed his wife's face. Closing her eyes, she spread her arms and parted her legs as wide as her crippled body allowed. She mumbled something he couldn't make out; he moved closer in the hope of understanding. She misunderstood his intention. "Yes, come closer. Now, I want to hear all the details."

"After I checked on the boy, I went to the side of the room and watched. Smoke, fog, I don't know what to call it, but it rose up from their bodies. The smoke was white, thin, and wispy, it hovered about five feet over them. All I could think of was that it was their souls. Then, the smoke disappeared. I'm not kidding, Irene, it was there one second and gone the next. I didn't know what was happening. I didn't know what to do. The kids looked the same, but I didn't dare check them after what you told me."

"Yes, you were instructed not to touch them, though you fucked that up already."

"I know," he said. "I didn't touch them, I stayed put and waited. About five minutes later, the smoke returned. It came down through the ceiling, slipping slowly, like snakes dropping from a tree. Only, the smoke was not white this time. It was black. There were two streams, thick, shiny-looking, like that jizz you're lying in."

She smiled at the comparison.

"The smoke-snakes got lower and lower, and moved over two of the girls. It went inside them, through their noses. It got sucked up into their bodies." He paused, recalling the image. "I waited a few minutes. Nothing else happened, so I went to check on the kids. The two girls the smoke went into were alive, I could see their chests moving up and down. The two boys and the other girl were dead. I checked their pulses."

Irene's hands went to her knees. She swept the palms over her thighs as she mumbled, "Two survived! That's better than I hoped for. I knew he needed to keep some of them, that's why we went with five."

When Irene had revealed she was studying the occult, he dismissed it as an odd phase she was going through. Over time, her occasional interest in the supernatural morphed into an obsession. Their conversations consisted of nothing but her studies. She continually brought up someone she called the Dark Master, a being she believed would grant her immortality and unnatural abilities. Though he tired of her constant comments about this mysterious guy, he put up with it. It was not as though he could stop her. He didn't know much about dementia, but he thought Irene might have been suffering from some form of it. Until the spooky stuff started happening.

Lights would turn on and off by themselves. Wall hangings dropped to the floor. Shadows slipped from corners. When alone, he would hear whispers. Irene would never express curiosity or surprise at the occurrences; at most, a slight grin served as an acknowledgment. While these events were strange, he considered them figments of his imagination at best, annoyances at worst. Then, shit got real.

Irene disappeared, and she was gone for four months.

Though he was tired of hearing her ramblings about the Dark Master, he had put up with it. He loved her, and up to the day she vanished, he thought the feeling was mutual. Throughout the many eccentricities Irene exhibited—the odd behavior, the strange occurrences—she continued to maintain their home and ensure their comfort. Sexual intimacy was in short supply, but that had never been high on her priority list anyway, though she was not above dispensing other forms of affection. Cuddling on the couch as they watched a show, hand-holding when they went for walks, and quick kisses on the lips were common, and welcomed. All that changed when those men took her.

Arriving home after work that evening, he had known something was wrong; it was as quiet as a tomb and the atmosphere as heavy. The living room furniture betrayed its age. In the dim light of dusk it looked tired, worn. A deep breath revealed another abnormality: the house smelled stale. Absent were the aromas of chicken, beef, or pasta. He cocked an ear in the hope of detecting the sounds of pots boiling, an oven door opening, or the slam of a cabinet, but silence pervaded. Fear chilled his thoughts. He crept toward the kitchen. It was empty. A search of the house proved the same. When she didn't return home by nine o'clock that evening, he called the police. Four months went by until a passing remark during a fight at the bar led him to her. Irene got her revenge on the four men that took her, but his involvement in their slaughter proved to be tacit approval in her participation in the dark arts. Now, he was her subordinate, and it scared the hell out of him.

EIGHT

Paul slumped on the couch, watching the local news. Cindy's disappearance was the top story, and it took all he had not to break down when they showed the photograph of his daughter that he had given the police. It had been taken months earlier, before her long blond hair had grown out, curls at the end brushing her shoulders.

He doubted he would learn anything from the coverage. Two days had passed since her abduction and the police had provided him with no new information.

To further the surreal nature of her kidnapping, the FBI had shown up yesterday afternoon. After consulting with local law enforcement, they briefed him before they left. Based on the previous four disappearances, they doubted a ransom was forthcoming, but common sense dictated they wiretap his phone. The landline had rung incessantly and he jumped like a startled rabbit every time. He answered each on the first ring, but the callers were usually relatives, friends, or news reporters. His responses to those he knew were the same in each instance—he had no further information, they should not come over, they should call back in a few days. His response to the news reporters was even briefer—he told them not to call back. Those who made it past the policeman stationed outside were turned away with a promise that he would keep them informed.

On the day Cindy was taken, his best friend and neighbor, Tom, received a call from his wife and he left work to join Paul. After finding Cindy's red barrette, and the subsequent interviews and searches, both men had rushed back into the woods, scouring for clues the police might have missed. At first, the detectives refused to let them into the woods, but after a lengthy and emotional argument, the cops relented, assigning an officer to accompany them. The three searched as far back as a quarter mile behind the house, but they found nothing. When it was too dark to continue, they reluctantly quit.

Arriving back at the house, Paul explained that he needed some time alone. In his bedroom with the door closed, he took a picture of Cindy, Chloe, and himself down from the wall. Pressing it to his chest, he whispered, "I'm sorry, Chloe." Sitting at the edge of his bed, Paul's shoulders shook and his chest hitched as the tears fell. He cried at the loss of his wife. He cried for Cindy. He cried about the carelessness that led him here.

Paul took some time to gather himself and clean up in the adjoining bathroom. After that, he went into the living room to thank Tom and send him home, though he refused to leave, insisting he stay with Paul through the night.

Time crawled. Paul dreaded every passing minute. He didn't need the authorities to tell him that the longer it took to find Cindy, the more likely she would meet a horrific end. If only time would stop completely. Every hour without word of his daughter boded more grief. His heart would race when the phone rang. If a detective came through the front door, his pulse would quicken. He would search the crowds gathered outside his house, looking for Cindy until his vision blurred.

Now, watching the evening news, his fright and guilt had turned to numbness and despair; his mind fogged from overthinking and a lack of sleep. The talking heads on television sounded distant. A glance at his friend revealed he had succumbed to exhaustion. Paul's head dipped, and less than a minute later, he lost his own battle against fatigue.

The landline's gentle ringtone violated the silence. It went on ringing until voice mail picked up. Twenty minutes later, Paul sat up with a start. Everything was out of focus. Trees, scrub brush, and an empty swing set shimmered through a haze. His daughter's arm, outstretched with a reaching for hand receded into a milky fog. Her screams faded into silence. A rapping sound, loud and persistent, echoed in his ears. His head swiveled toward it. After several seconds, he pulled his thoughts together enough to remember he was in his own bed. The rapping continued on, louder, with more rapidity. *THUMP THUMP THUMP.*

Someone was knocking on his front door.

Sighing, he shook away the remnants of his dream. Tom, yawning, mumbled something Paul couldn't make out. Paul's attention snapped back to the incessant rapping, because this time it was followed with a plea.

"Mr. Lane, please open up, I'm from the Goffstown Police Department."

Paul was wide awake now.

Must be bad news. Why else would they be coming to his house in the middle of the night? *Wait. Is it still night?* A glance at the window revealed daylight—he had slept through the night. Approaching the front door, he anticipated the worst. Opening it, Captain Bechtel stood at the top of the stairs. His face was neutral and Paul didn't know if that was a good or a bad sign.

"What is it, Officer?"

"Mr. Lane. We've found Cindy. She's alive."

NINE

Long after the police had removed his handcuffs, Manuel's wrists continued to ache. Sitting on the thin foam sheet that served as a mattress, he massaged them. The cot, bolted to the floor, was the only item in the jail room. His bathroom needs were met with a portable toilet, wheeled into the cell twice a day; his meals were pushed through a small space underneath the bars; communication was limited. Simple commands such as *sit, shit,* and *go to the cot* were the extent of the conversations.

The portable toilet was humiliating. After leaving the stainless-steel receptacle, the cops would retreat from his cell, slide the door closed, and observe him. The tasers they held made it clear that he had better not try anything funny, though he had no idea what they would consider funny. Too embarrassed to use the tarnished device they left with him, he couldn't find it in him to go. His refusal to eat the slop they served up helped in that regard. A full day had passed since his arrest, too long to go without food, and now he was hungry enough to eat the watery powdered eggs and spam-like meat shoved through the hole at the bottom of his door. As he shoveled the food into his mouth using the only utensil they provided—a pressed cardboard spoon—he had a hunch he would not say *no* next time when it came to the portable toilet.

Manuel had yet to see a lawyer, despite promises. They also ignored his requests to speak with the captain, and his demand for a phone call. Shouted pleas went unanswered or even acknowledged, leaving him to believe he was the jail's only occupant.

A ceiling camera outside his cell watched Manuel's every move. He took to staring at it, talking to it, and making hand gestures to attract attention. It was futile. Frustration set in. The urge to throw something at the camera was fierce, only they had taken away all his possessions. Reduced to sitting on the cot wearing an orange jumpsuit, he analyzed his situation constantly, his thoughts uninterrupted except for meal offerings, rants at the camera, proffered bathroom breaks, and whatever sleep he could manage.

How could they think I killed those missing children? What evidence could they have? He needed to learn more. Why wasn't a lawyer appointed to him? Why were the police stalling?

Thoughts of Ms. Delaney floated into his head. *I was at her home investigating her husband before they arrested me. Could it have been a coincidence? Was her seduction part of all this?*

Manuel caught himself. He wasn't seduced. If anything, he had pursued the woman, but for the life of him, he couldn't understand why. A cold shiver danced down his spine. There was no doubt even the horniest teenager would have had second thoughts bedding Ms. Delaney. Yet, in a few instances at her home, he had thought her attractive—enough so to kiss her and let her perform oral sex on him. He tried to recall what she looked like when he was burning with desire for her, but the mental picture eluded him. Her body was out of focus, a grayish blur. Her face had no features.

The sound of keys jangling and a tumbler turning broke his concentration. Seconds later, the squeak of hinges from down the hall filled the air. Voices—two men having a conversation; the echo of their footsteps followed. Reaching his cell, he recognized one of them—Captain Bechtel—but the other man was unfamiliar to him.

"Mr. Chance, this is Wade Thompson, your court-appointed attorney," the captain said without preamble. "We can do this one of two ways," he continued. "The first is to take you upstairs into a room and restrain you. You will be seated in a chair, your ankles and wrists bound, secured with chains to the floor. You will have privacy, and a guard will be outside the room. Or, you can conduct business in your cell, with your attorney on this side of the bars. The door to your cell will remain locked. An armed guard posted nearby must inspect any and all items passed to you. If this rule is broken, the meeting will be terminated. Your conversations are subject to attorney-client privilege and will remain confidential and thus cannot be used in a court of law."

Manuel's first impulse was to stay in the cell. He had no idea where this "room" was, and despite the captain's assurances, he pictured a large mirror on one of the walls with crowds of investigators watching and listening to him from the other side. He had nothing to hide, but the indignity of appearing in restraints and a prison jumpsuit in front of others was too much for him to bear. On the other hand, it would be nice to get out of his cell, even under those circumstances. He decided to ask the attorney.

"Mr. Thompson, do you have a preference?"

The attorney appraised Manuel before replying directly to the officer. "We can conduct our business here."

The captain nodded. "Hang on a minute." He walked away from the jail cell and returned with an aluminum stool and another officer on his heels. "You know the drill, Wade," Bechtel said. "You and the stool stay out of arm's reach. If you need to pass something to him, call Officer Watts here to examine it first. You've got an hour."

As soon as Wade Thompson sat down, Manuel peppered him with questions and protestations. "What the hell is all this about? Why do they think I took those kids? I've never hurt anyone in my life, never mind a kid. You've got to get me out of here!"

"Whoa, Mr. Chance. First, let me get our business in order." The attorney spent the next five minutes explaining his part in the proceedings and the financial arrangements.

Manuel sighed. "I am not a wealthy man, Mr. Thompson, and I understand your service is covered by the county. I do not have a lawyer, and to be honest, I wouldn't know how to get one that specialized in this kind of thing, never mind afford one. You're all I've got, so let's get on with this."

"Okay, Mr. Chance—"

"Call me Manny."

"Sure. Well, Manny, let's start with the charge that landed you here. You are being held on suspicion of three counts of kidnapping. Murder charges are pending. An anonymous male phoned the Goffstown Police Department and reported suspicious activity at an address that proved to be your home. A single cruiser with two patrol officers arrived and surveilled the premises. They discovered the back door to your house open. After failed attempts to call the occupier to the door, they entered the premises to do a well-being check. Entering the master bedroom, they discovered scraps of clothing with bloodstains. The officers recognized that the clothing matched the descriptions of some of the outfits the missing children were last seen wearing. They radioed in their findings. Backup arrived, along with detectives."

Manuel was stunned. *This can't be happening. I've got nothing to do with those missing kids.* "You've got to believe me, Mr. Thompson, I have no idea how that clothing got into my house. I didn't take those kids. Someone set me up. It's obvious."

His attorney remained quiet. When he spoke, he looked into Manuel's eyes. "Yeah. It's got the feel of a setup. I've brought this up to Captain Bechtel, and while he didn't agree with the assessment, he didn't deny it, either. The FBI is involved in the case, and they'll investigate this aspect also. On the face of this alone, we would have a strong argument for bond."

"Wait. Bond? On the face of this alone? What else is going on here?"

"Mr. Chance, you are also being held on suspicion of forcible rape."

Manuel froze. Rape? Oh no. God, no.

"Manny, are you familiar with a Ms. Delaney?"

His shoulders sunk. Closing his eyes, he lowered his head, muttering, "My God, this is so wrong." He lifted his head and addressed his attorney. "Yes, I do know Ms. Delaney. I visited with her yesterday. We did have oral sex, but it was not rape. It was consensual. She said it was rape?"

"She did, Manny. Yesterday afternoon, she arrived at an emergency room in Manchester, asking for assistance, claiming you had sexually assaulted her. An examination ensued and a semen sample acquired. An arrest warrant was issued. The attorney general's office is comparing a DNA analysis of the sample with biological evidence taken from your house. You can expect the AG to ask you for another sample from your person."

Manuel's mouth dropped. "This doesn't make sense. She performed oral sex on me. I never had intercourse with her." Then it hit him. He thought she didn't care for the taste of semen so she spit it out into a glass. She saved it. Saved it for proof that he had raped her.

"Mr. Wade, I was at Ms. Delaney's house at her invitation. She was concerned that her husband was involved in the kidnappings. She promised to give me her story if I looked around her property for any evidence that he might have taken those kids. I was thinking she was so grateful for helping her out, she performed oral sex on me."

The attorney eyebrows lifted. "Manny, that's your story?"

"Yes! It's the truth."

Wade sighed. "Okay, let's start at the beginning…"

TEN

"Mr. Lane," Captain Bechtel repeated, "Cindy is alive."

Torn between an emotional pull to weep and the need to learn more, Paul shook in the doorway. *I need to focus, find out where she's at, how she is. I can cry later.* "How is she? Is she okay?"

"All I can say, sir, is that she is alive and in good hands."

"Wait," Paul replied, "Alive and in good hands? Has she been harmed?"

"Sir, all I can only tell you is what I know, and that's all I've been told."

"I need to see her. Now!"

Pointing to the street, the officer said, "We have a cruiser parked outside to bring you to her."

Paul stole a quick glance to Tom.

Wide-eyed, Tom motioned for him to get going, and added, "I'll stay here, keep an eye on things."

Not bothering to grab his wallet or keys, Paul rushed out the door. When he arrived at the cruiser, he pulled the rear door open but stopped short of entering. Lynne Carole was in the back seat. They made uneasy eye contact. Streaks of black liner trailed down her cheeks and her eyes were wet. Lynne spoke first. "They found our babies."

"Your daughter, Lisa? They found her, too?"

"Yes."

"And she's safe?"

"Yes. I don't know about the other three."

Paul scrambled through the door and sat next to Lynne. Captain Bechtel slid into the driver's seat. As the cruiser took off, Paul placed his elbows on his knees, and lowered his head until his hands cupped his face. Though his shoulders shook, his sobs were gentle. Lynne eased closer and wrapped an arm around him. Neither spoke until they arrived at CMC Hospital.

Paul's mouth dropped when he realized where they were. "Cindy's here? Is she hurt?"

Captain Bechtel raised his gaze to his rearview mirror. "She did not appear to be hurt. When we found her and Lisa, we brought them here for a physical evaluation. They've been here for over two hours now, and the last I heard, they seem to be physically okay."

Lynne shot back. "Two hours? You had them here for two hours and you didn't tell us?"

"We had to make sure they were your children. Look, we need to go inside and discuss this. It can't be done out here."

It was Paul's turn to jump on him. "Make sure they were our children? Something's wrong, isn't there? You're not telling us something. I want to know what the hell is going on!"

The officer sighed. He got out of the cruiser and opened Lynne's door. "Come on, we'll finish this inside."

They rode the elevator to the second floor. The captain directed them to a room, empty but for three chairs. A curtain took up half of one wall. They each took a seat, and Bechtel stared at the ceiling for a moment before addressing them.

"Approximately two and a half hours ago, we got a phone call from a woman on Pattie Hill Road. She said there were two children, girls, who were walking down the road without any adults nearby. She stopped and asked them where their parents were. The girls appeared calm, claimed they were lost, trying to get home. A patrol car arrived minutes later, and the officer recognized the two girls as those among the missing. He radioed in and was instructed to bring them here. I hurried down and met with my counterpart of the Manchester Police Department. After the girls passed a preliminary evaluation, we talked with them. We confirmed their identity, but there is some confusion. Before I bring you to them, I need you to confirm they are your daughters."

"I—I don't understand," Lynne said, "Did something bad happen to them? Are they disfigured somehow?"

Captain Bechtel's hands flew up. "No, no, nothing like that. As I said, they appear to be fine, in good health." Pointing to the curtain, he added, "They're in the next room, playing with toys. I'm going to draw this back so you can see them. I don't want to cause you any more stress if they are not who we think they are, so tell me if they're your daughters."

Paul and Lynne jumped from their chairs. Paul didn't wait for the captain to draw the curtain. He reached for an end and yanked, sliding it to the side. He gasped, and Lynne broke down in tears. Both their daughters were sitting on the floor playing with toys. Animated, they twirled plastic horses and dolls while chatting with each other. When Paul's heart stopped hammering, he studied his daughter for any signs of physical abuse. He saw nothing to cause him alarm. "Yes, that's Cindy."

Lynne managed, "And that's my baby," between sobs.

Captain Bechtel's face tightened. "Okay, now could you point..."

He didn't have a chance to finish the sentence. The girls caught sight of their parents in the window. They squealed and waved. The adults ran to the door, opened it, and hurried to the one on the other side of the glass. Once inside, they crouched by the door, arms wide to welcome their daughters. The girls screamed in delight, dropped their toys, and ran into their arms.

Lisa wrapped her tiny arms around Paul's neck. "Daddy!" She purred into his ear.

Cindy hugged Lynne tight and wouldn't let go. "Mommy, you found me!"

Paul's eyes met Lynne's. She was as confused as he was. He reached out to Cindy who clung to Lynne's neck and placed a hand on the child's shoulder. "Cindy, I'm over here." The girl shrank away from his touch

A reply came from the other girl, buried in his arms. "I know, Daddy, never leave me alone again."

Lynne pulled the blond-haired girl hanging from her neck and held the child out as far as her arms would allow. She stared into the girl's eyes. "Cindy?"

The child scrunched her face. "Why are you calling me that, Mommy? You know my name is Lisa."

Once more, Paul's gaze focused on Lynne. Her body was rigid. Eyes wide, she focused her stare on him. *Terror, her eyes are wide with terror.* The girl in Lynne's arms—his daughter, Cindy—slowly rotated her head toward him. When their eyes locked, the child grinned.

ELEVEN

Manuel had attended pre-trial hearings as a reporter, never dreaming that he would be on the other side of the gallery. After the prosecutor made his case, he invited Captain Bechtel to provide additional information. To Manuel's relief, Bechtel testified that the evidence might be considered suspect.

"Your honor, the only evidence in this case is a result of an anonymous tip-off. When we arrived at the scene, the rear door of the residence was open, the evidence out in plain sight. We found nothing else to indicate the defendant's involvement other than the clothing."

The judge acknowledged his testimony with a simple, "Go on."

"In addition, two of the abducted children have been found. They have not tied the defendant to their kidnapping."

The judge raised his eyebrows.

"In addition, the defendant has no criminal record. He owns the local newspaper, and up to now has been considered an asset to the community."

Bechtel then addressed the rape case.

"The evidence in the sexual assault charge is not suspect as the DNA analysis confirmed it was the defendant's. However, there is a question as to whether the act was consensual, and we are investigating this."

The judge sat back. "So, you're telling me that the defendant could have possibly been set up in both the abduction and the sexual assault cases?"

"At this time, we don't know. But, yes, there might be a suspicious connection between the two crimes. We are investigating in co-ordination with the New Hampshire Attorney General's Office and the FBI."

The judge called the prosecutor and Manuel's attorney to the bench. After a brief discussion, the judge ruled.

"The prosecutor has agreed to release the defendant provided he does not travel outside the town. Bail is set at twenty thousand dollars."

With the bang of a gavel, the hearing was over. Manuel was relieved that bail was set, but the amount concerned him. He had no choice but to use the equity in his home to cover it with the bondsman. After filling out the necessary paperwork, he followed up with his attorney in a conference room in the courthouse.

His lawyer briefed him about the discovery of the missing children.

"Two of them were found. Cindy and Lisa. The police wasted no time in talking to them and showing them your photograph. Neither of the girls identified you. They said they had never seen you before. I asked Bechtel if the kids described their kidnapper. He shook his head. The descriptions they gave were vague, of no help."

"Thank God two of them were found. Any word on the other three?" asked Manuel.

"No. I'm sure he's as baffled over all of this as you are. "From what I know of Captain Bechtel," Manuel said, "he's a good man. He'll work this case until he figures it out. He said something about a suspicious connection. He has to be talking about Mrs. Delaney, right?"

"Yeah. Bechtel and I had an unusually candid conversation about her. He remarked that Delaney had gone through a traumatic event involving her own abduction and multiple rapes. Those acts could be affecting her judgment. He didn't go into detail, but he hinted that the woman was withholding information in her case."

Manuel sighed. "How could I have been so stupid to get involved with her?"

"Don't be so hard on yourself. You're a reporter. You were doing your job. You should also know that Bechtel confided to me that he has interacted with you professionally and socially in the past. His gut told him you were not a kidnapper or a rapist."

Wade concluded their meeting and Manuel set up an appointment with the lawyer for the following week. After shaking hands, Manuel stepped outside the courthouse. Though the air was cool and dry, it was as welcome as a tropical breeze. An odor of freshly cut grass assailed his nostrils. He took it in, holding his breath. He vowed never to take that smell for granted again. Exhaling, he stared at the ground.

I know I keep asking myself, but how the hell did all this happen?

On his way home, he replayed the series of events that had led him to this point. Attention to his surroundings turned to autopilot as images of Duck Lady passed through his mind.

A movement in his peripheral vision stopped him cold.

It was a shadow. Large. Indistinct. When he concentrated on where he had seen it, there was nothing there. Scanning the area revealed nothing. He attributed the vision to nerves and continued homeward. Twice more it happened. Approaching his house, he couldn't shake the feeling that someone was watching him. Following him. Maybe stalking him. Back stiffening, he hurried his pace until he reached the front doorstep. Yellow crime-scene tape ripped off easily. Crumpling it into a ball, he threw it to the ground. Digging keys from his pocket, he placed his other hand on the doorknob. The door pushed open an inch at his touch. He hesitated, but only briefly. He wanted to get inside as quickly as possible. He stepped through and locked the door behind him. Spinning, he put his back to the door. Eyes trained on the living room, his breath caught in his chest.

Furniture lay on its side, coffee and end tables were upside down, stuffing was strewn everywhere from ripped-open cushions. Lamps were in pieces, as was his television set. Glass and debris littered the floor. The kitchen had fared no better. The front door had been unlocked and he supposed the back door was also. Could the police have done this, or did vandals cause all this damage?

There was no avoiding the mess on the floor as he made his way to the staircase, the sounds of crunching glass accompanying him. He needed to lie down in his own bed if possible. Exhausted, he craved sleep. Reaching the top step, he turned left and entered his bedroom.

Once more, his breath caught in his chest.

Though the room had been ransacked, the bed was made, untouched.

Irene Delaney sat on the end of it.

The woman was naked—a living portrait, painted black. Tattoos in constant motion slithered over her body. Symbols, glyphs, and odd lettering slunk around her legs, crisscrossed her torso, only to reach her neck and then make their way back down. Her flesh defined their canvas. He remembered her hair as dark with streaks of gray, but now it was a shock of white. Her eyes, perfect ovals, absorbed the darkness of the room. They were as black as tar. Her smile boasted yellow teeth, a slightly darker shade than her face, feet, and hands. "Welcome home, Manny," she teased.

"What the fuck are you?"

Her smile faded. "I am still Irene Delaney, but soon I will be much more. I've summoned the Dark Master, and he has chosen me to stand by his side, to help him return to this world. He needs something. A box. It contains the souls of his brothers, his sisters—his soldiers. Once he is in possession of the box, he will make our world his, and I will stake my place in it."

She's fucking nuts.

He would not have accepted her ramblings as truth if he hadn't spent the last few days in jail for crimes he didn't commit. Not to mention that she had somehow coerced him sexually. Maybe she was a witch, or maybe she wasn't human. Considering she was now sitting in front of him with tattoos dancing over her body, it didn't matter what the hell she was—she defied logic. It was as if he were in some bizarre dream. Only, no amount of screaming and pleading with himself to wake up would get him out of this nightmare. Why was she here spouting all this nonsense about dark masters and a freaking box? What did all that have to do with him? He was scared shitless and had no idea what to do. Gathering the courage to talk, he said, "If what you say is true, let that Dark Man get the damned box himself."

"It's Dark Master, not Dark Man. I don't know his real name yet."

"I don't care what you call him. Why in the world would you want to summon him in the first place?"

Irene smirked. "Manny, I first called him over five months ago. Those four boys didn't kidnap me. I recruited them." She pushed her shoulder forward, highlighting her deformed back while running her fingers over her tattoos. "They did all this to me at my urging. The demon I called for responds only to pain and sacrifice."

"Even if you believe all of this, why would you put yourself through all that torture? And why would you want to hurt me? Hurt others?"

"Manny, isn't it obvious? Power. I want power."

Manuel grimaced. "What do I have to do with all of this?"

"You have a newspaper, Manny. It will serve as a way to pave the way for us. It can divert suspicion. It will promote and normalize us while we plan, while we build up our strength. Your paper is small, perfect for seeding. As you print more about us, people will come to accept what is happening, what *will* happen. The larger news outlets will pick up on it."

"Why here? Why Goffstown?"

She leaned toward him. "The box the Dark Master seeks is here, in Goffstown, located in a pawnshop. Its guardian has prevented our attempt to procure it. One effort to retrieve it has failed. We will need a less obvious, more pedestrian way to retrieve the box. We will use you, Manny."

Manuel stepped back. "There's no way I'm going to use my newspaper to help you. As for using me to search for some damn box to build some fucking occult army, forget about it. I'm leav..." His words cut off in mid-sentence. His mind clouded. Eyes blinking, he attempted to shake the feeling. The weight in his mind traveled to his shoulders. His breathing slowed as he slumped.

He fought against the fog in his head. His chin rose, and he stared at Irene.

She looked different.

Sitting on the bed, he once again appreciated how attractive she was. Her beauty would rival that of any model. Her complexion was smooth, creamy, rich in color. A petite nose, full lips, and doe-eyes competed for his attention. Breasts, full, round, and firm, begged to be fondled. Her nipples were erect. Inviting. Her waist was small, tight, her figure shaped like an hourglass. Legs long and sleek were folded, leading to small, delicate feet.

He shook his head. This couldn't be real. He'd been through this before. She had to be a witch. He knew better than to believe what he was seeing, though the compulsion to take her was no less potent than the last time. In fact, it was greater.

Irene unfolded her legs. Placing her hands on her thighs, she pushed them aside. Her legs spread wide, exposing her sex. The entrance gaped. It was dark, with a darker fluid trickling down onto the bedspread. "Manny, I pleased you the last time we met. It's your turn to please me, now. Come, taste me."

Desire overwhelmed him. He stepped toward her. Irene tilted her head back. The space between her legs widened. Manuel heard a soft moaning as her mouth opened. She cooed, "Yes, come closer."

In the lusty fog of his mind, he saw an image of himself. It raged at him to stop—this was wrong, evil, it screamed—imploring that it would be the end of him. Yet, the compulsion to go to her was too strong. He couldn't resist. He didn't want to resist. He approached her.

He was on his knees, inches from her crotch. The liquid leaking from her oozed black, its odor sweet. Licking his lips, he leaned forward.

Pain ripped through his head.

Fingers gripped his scalp, twisted, and pulled. His gaze flew to the ceiling. The smell of rot attacked his nostrils. A man's face slipped into his view. The head was so large it obscured everything else.

Manuel was pulled up and back. His knees lifted from the floor as he sailed through the air. Seconds later, the pain in his head vanished, replaced with an anguished jolt in his back. Landing on something hard, his hands flailed. It took him a moment to realize he was lying on the floor. His head cleared, and the view before him left him wondering if he was hallucinating.

The biggest man he had ever seen in his life stood to the side of Irene Delaney. The woman, her legs still spread wide on the ebony-stained bedspread, was enraged. Her eyes reverted to their previous inky depth, penetrating the giant with their malevolence. The woman's mouth opened wider than possible, a screech vomiting from her throat. The giant's right arm drew back, making a fist. It shot forward.

The fist never made contact. Irene's body vanished, and the brute's arm passed through thin air.

Manuel's mouth dropped, but the giant seemed to take her disappearance in stride. He shrugged his shoulders as if it were to be expected. His nonchalance was temporary. "You need to come with me," he said, turning to Manuel.

"You—you saved me. Who are you?"

The man's voice was coarse. "Rex."

"How—how did you know what was happening?"

The giant extended a hand and lifted Manuel off the floor. "I was following you."

"You were following me?" Realization hit. "It was you I kept seeing out of the corner of my eye. You followed me from the courthouse. But why?"

What passed for a frown spread across the giant's lips. "I was going to kill you."

Manuel shivered. "Kill me? Why?"

"I don't like men who hurt children."

"But, I didn't hurt anyone!"

The giant nodded. "I believe you. Come with me if you want to live."

"Want to live? What's that mean? Why should I come with you?"

"You need to talk to someone."

"Who?"

As he walked out of the bedroom, the giant said, "The pawnshop owner."

TWELVE

In the past four months, while deep in the bowels of the Catholic Church building in Haverhill, Massachusetts, Father MacLeod had conducted the exorcism rites on Celeste twenty-five times without success.

This afternoon's attempt yielded similar results.

Defeated, depressed, he pulled at his beard three times before placing the exorcism ritual book on a small table in the corner of the room. Removing a chair from beneath the table, he dragged it over the concrete floor to the woman's bedside to assess his failure. His first thought as he sat by her side was always the same: *Celeste, where the hell are you?*

Unlike all the other exorcisms he had performed, Celeste's appearance hadn't changed since she had been brought here from the Moore House. After all this time, the woman should have been unrecognizable—a living cadaver adorned with infected sores covering her body, and facial features gruesome enough to induce nausea. The usual odor from the possessed was non-existent in her case. In another odd twist, the room smelled faintly of flowers—*lilacs,* he often thought. Her weight should have been less than eighty pounds, and by all rights, the outlines of her bones should have been visible through her skin. Yet her body mass had remained stable over the last four months, despite sustenance consisting solely of nutrients from an IV. Her complexion was smooth, healthy enough to reflect the light of the florescent bulbs hanging from the ceiling. Rosy cheeks mirrored her lips. With the exception of clear tubes and medical bags attached to accept waste, she lay on the bed wrapped only in a thin blanket. Though her wrists and ankles were bound to the bed frame, she exhibited no chafing or ligature marks. Equally baffling, bedsores were non-existent. Father MacLeod couldn't help but marvel at her condition. The woman was beautiful; you'd never know she was possessed by a demon.

As he gazed at Celeste, carnal thoughts broke through the priest's subconscious. The resulting erection was uncomfortable.

The reaction was inevitable. It occurred every time he concluded the ritual. He justified it by telling himself it was the demon's work, its way of taunting him for his failures. He had no proof of this, but to think otherwise would compound his guilt. To challenge that belief would acknowledge how low his moral barometer actually was. No matter the reason, he had not succumbed to the temptation before him—not yet anyway. Instead of acting on those impulses, the priest used them to his advantage. He stored the sensations, the images, the suppressed violations in his head. He would then recall them, add to them as he travelled to a brothel in New Hampshire. There, he could release his pent-up lust, act on those sinful passions, and take comfort that he had thwarted the demon once more.

Rising from the chair, he adjusted himself. There was a nun outside the doorway who not only acted as a sentry, but also administered care to Celeste. The last thing he wanted was to make Sister Bernice aware of his arousal, though he supposed there were times he was unable to hide it.

He recalled one instance when Sister Bernice had flown into the room as he exited. He backtracked moments later to see the nun inspecting Celeste's genitalia, then the unconscious woman's mouth. The urge to reprimand the nun was strong. She understood the power of the demon, what it was capable of, but there should have been no doubt in her mind that as a priest, he could resist the demon's pull. The nun should have been certain he would never violate Celeste in that way. Standing outside that doorway that day, he had let the matter go, and resumed the walk back to his office. Though loath to admit it at the time, a part of him was grateful for the nun's reaction.

The chair legs screeched along the floor as he returned it to the table. The ritual book in hand, he proceeded to the door. As his fingers pushed the numbers on the keypad, he stopped short. Fingers frozen, he heard a voice silenced four months earlier.

"Father MacLeod."

Leaning forward, his forehead rested on the door. His jaw tightened as his shoulders stiffened. Who had called him? Was it Celeste, or the demon possessing her? Her healthy physical condition suggested the former, but as he had learned from prior possessions, the demon would allow the host some freedom if it served its purpose.

"Father MacLeod, I know you can hear me."

The priest inhaled, twisted his neck to view the bed.

Celeste's eyes were open, the corners of her lips curled into a smile. The first word that popped into his head was *angelic*. Shame weighed on him as he recalled his earlier thoughts. He straightened and stepped toward her. "Celeste?"

The woman's smile widened and her eyes brightened. "No."

Father MacLeod winced, and his heart hammered. He raised the book in his hand and held it out before him. "Who are you?"

"You know who I am, Father."

MacLeod's voice rose. "How about you placate me, demon?"

"I am James Moore."

He had suspected as much, but hearing it from the woman's lips aggravated the ache in his soul. MacLeod's attempts to exorcise the demon inside Celeste revolved around it being Moore. His repeated failures had him questioning if this was true, or if there were more than one demon possessing her.

Celeste had saved so many lives at the Moore House four months earlier, including his, when she took the demon, James Moore, inside herself. Not a day went by that he didn't imagine the horror and the fear she must be struggling with. The demon's answer revealed that those nightmare scenarios might not be figments of his imagination. Guilt crushed him with the weight of a boulder. He addressed the demon in a soft, pleading tone. "Why don't you leave this woman alone and go back to Hell where you belong?"

The demon's smile faltered as the light in its host's eyes dimmed. "You would have to ask Celeste that."

Startled, the priest said, "Explain yourself."

"It's not Celeste who is captive, priest. It's me."

Father MacLeod stared at the woman, lust now the furthest thing from his mind. His thoughts raced as he wrapped his mind around the statement. Celeste, not the demon, was the captor? If so, to what purpose was she refusing to relinquish her hold on it? Could she still be protecting him and the team who had defeated Moore?

"Why," MacLeod asked, "would she hold on to you?"

"A better question might be, priest, is why she's letting me talk to you now."

Father MacLeod's back stiffened. If it were true, if she *was* holding on to the soul of James Moore, there could only be one reason Celeste was willing to relinquish a small portion of control. She wanted to warn MacLeod about something—something big enough to take that risk. There was a problem with this, though. Why would the demon agree to assist Celeste? There had to be something in it for James Moore. Between the two, a deal of some kind must have been worked out. The priest sighed. If this were true, no good would come of it. Not only were demons liars, they were tricky, and there was a good chance Celeste would suffer a fate worse than the one she was experiencing now if she wasn't careful. It seemed the die was cast, however, and he owed it to Celeste to at least listen to the demon. After a few more moments of thought, he responded, "If she is indeed allowing you to speak to me, then say what you will, just know I've been played by a demon before and I don't intend to let it happen again."

"Wife-fucker, you might have doubts concerning the reasons for this *tête-à-tête*, but let me assure you, I am only doing this because I have something to gain."

Father MacLeod's head reared back at the term *wife-fucker*. Having sex with James Moore's wife when the demon was human was an act of convenience. He had been counseling the woman on family issues when the opportunity to bed her had presented itself. She was willing—how could he pass it up? Images of the woman materialized in his mind. As he thought about her, regret took seed. If he had had the good sense not to screw her in her own home, they wouldn't have been caught, and Moore wouldn't have flipped out. The man

89

wouldn't have embraced demonism, killed his wife and child, and caused bloody havoc at the Moore House. For some reason, the priest had never put it all together until now, that *he* was the reason all those people had suffered and died. The realization stunned him and his knees went weak. He glanced over at Celeste. Her eyes were bright. Her stare penetrated his, and a cruel smile adorned her lips. *I can't let this fucker get to me!* Now was not the time to analyze past sins. He buried the images and their implications and concentrated on the matter at hand. He steeled himself and spoke. "Get on with it."

"There is an item you are to retrieve. It's called the Prexy Box. You are to acquire it, and then do with it as instructed."

The priest's face tightened. "What?"

The smile on Celeste's face faltered. "Hell is not unlike this living plane. It has factions, and they are constantly vying for more power. Lucifer rules with an iron fist, but there is always someone who covets the position. Attempts at betrayal are few, but there's always a demon who believes they deserve the right to rule over Hell. At present, it is a demon that goes by the cliché-ridden nickname of the Dark Master. I cannot say its name aloud, priest, the last thing you want to do is call it here. This demon's controlling faction in Hell is strengthening; it is now a threat. The Dark Master has gone into hiding; even Lucifer cannot find him. Both have their allies, but Lucifer has the upper hand at present. But, if this Dark Master manages to get many more demons on its side, well, as the saying goes, all hell could break loose."

"You expect me to believe this? I have no idea what the hell a Prexy Box is, never mind how to find one. But I'm not stupid enough to fall for it. This is a trick, and you want this box for your own fucked-up purposes. How the hell did you get Celeste to buy into this?"

Celeste's body moved. The blanket flew off her and onto the floor. Her arm jettisoned the IV and the tubes that evacuated waste from her orifices. Dark stains expanded on the mattress. The restraints on all four of her limbs snapped; her legs slipped off the side of the bed, then she stood. Months of immobility had left her muscles weak and she rocked back and forth in an attempt to gain balance. Seconds later, she froze, focused on the priest, and then stepped forward. Unsteady, she shuffled toward him. Though stunned, he stood his ground. When they were almost nose to nose, she halted. He couldn't pull his eyes away from hers. Her sockets were lifeless, dark tunnels that stretched into infinity. The odor from the leaking waste tubes slammed into his nostrils and an urge to vomit overcame him. He took advantage of this distraction and stepped back.

"If it brings you comfort, wife-fucker, I will not harm you. Celeste has me by the balls and will not allow it. Know this, priest, this will not always be the case. One day, I *will* come for you, whether you are alive or dead."

Father MacLeod remained silent, though his wide eyes spoke volumes, betraying fear.

"I'm going to explain all of this to you, and you'd better listen. Like I told you, I have a stake in this, so does Celeste. So do you. This Dark Master needs the souls of demons not bound by Hell to tip the scale of war in his favor. The Prexy Box holds those souls. If he can free them, they will serve him."

Uncertainty filled the priest. "Why doesn't Lucifer take those souls himself?"

"There is an understanding between God and Lucifer to allow life on the living plane to reach its preordained result. Your God takes a dim view of anyone who fucks around with his plan. Skirmishes such as the one at my house are allowed as they provide Him amusement, as long as they are inconsequential to the inevitable conclusion."

Father MacLeod interrupted. "Inevitable conclusion? You mean where our souls go after death?"

"Yes. All is predetermined. There is a balance of power—of sorts. While your God is dominant, there were eras when Lucifer came close, but close is as far as it gets. Your God would never allow Lucifer the upper hand, let alone equality. If Lucifer acquired the souls in the Prexy Box, it would be seen as an attempt to upset the balance. Lucifer's punishment would be swift. He would cease to exist. Hell would cease to exist. Without Hell, there would be no need for demons. Without Hell, the fear of God would be unnecessary. What if, in the afterlife, there were no consequences for your actions? Why would..."

The priest broke in. "Let me guess, since it's predetermined and we don't have to work at getting God's approval, why bother with us in the first place?"

The demon nodded.

Father MacLeod retreated further from the demon, stopped, and pulled on his beard. "Let's say I believe all of that. Why am I supposed to be the one to grab this box, and what am I supposed to do with it?"

"The *why* benefits you directly. It seems you are in debt to one of us. You owe him a soul. Shall I say his name out loud? Prod your memory?"

The priest lowered his gaze and shook his head. "No. I remember. There's no need to call him."

Years ago, in order to save his nephew's life, Father MacLeod had made a deal with a demon named Asmodeus. The bargain called for two souls to Asmodeus in exchange for the young boy's life, but the priest had only delivered on half the deal. As jaded as the cleric was with the Catholic Church, the seeds of his faith had deep roots. Guilt and remorse weighed heavily on his soul after he led a homeless man into Asmodeus' clutches. The man's death was so horrific, MacLeod vowed not honor the remainder of the bargain. Asmodeus wasn't amused. The demon had since made one threatening overture at the priest when he visited a brothel in New Hampshire. The end result of that confrontation went in Father MacLeod's favor due to a supernatural necklace he was given.

The demon continued. "Asmodeus will void your deal if you assist us with obtaining the Prexy Box. If you are successful, and you follow the instructions given, Celeste will release me back to Hell, and she will return to this living plane."

Father MacLeod gazed at his shoes. He lifted his head and responded. "I was going to say, what the hell is the point in all this if everything is preordained? But, I think I know what your answer would be. Free will. We make the choices that lead us to whatever is waiting. Though our destiny is determined, the path we choose is equally as important as the end result. Or some shit like that."

The demon turned from Father MacLeod and stepped toward Celeste's bed. "I'm surprised you are capable of understanding, priest. Maybe you're not as dumb as I thought you were." She lay down on the bed, placing her hands near the top corners and spreading her legs wide. The faint smell of lilacs vanished. "Grab the Prexy Box; once you have it, instructions will be provided to you."

"I do have one last question. If this Dark Master is so powerful, why doesn't it possess a posse, a bar full of people, or a small army to grab the box?"

The demon laughed. "I take it back, you are as dumb as I thought. You've been an exorcist for years; how many times have you seen multiple possessions at once? It takes time to possess the living, and we are bound to that person once we have taken them over. What we do is possess the recently deceased or innocent souls that have been selected or sacrificed in our name. We can feed on them, sentence them to torment, or return the soul to their bodies with our essence imbedded. I don't mind saying, that's the fun part. But, there is a limit on how far we can stretch ourselves."

The priest mulled this over. "What you're saying is that if I do this, I won't have to fight off a whole company of possessed truck drivers coming after me?"

"No. The biggest threat will be the one the Dark Master has initially chosen as the vessel. He will use other demons, lesser demons to possess any accomplices. So, there could be—will be—other innocents who have been sacrificed or chosen that he will manipulate. But, priest, I have no doubt someone as conniving and vile as you will figure it all out."

"You just said I was dumb."

"You are. Dumb as a fox. In the meantime, priest, how about you fuck Celeste? I won't harm you, and I can assure you, she would delight in some earthly stimulation."

Father MacLeod gazed at the young woman's body. In other circumstances, he would have leapt at the chance. This was not one of those times. "You can't tempt me, demon." He paused for a moment, knowing the statement was only partially true. "If I agree to this arrangement, you say that my deal with Asmodeus will be fulfilled, Celeste will release you back to Hell, and she will return to us."

"Yes."

"Where is this Prexy Box you keep referencing?"

A grin formed on Celeste's lips. "It's in the possession of a caretaker. Someone you know quite well."

"Who?"

"Your friend, the pawnshop owner."

Father MacLeod punched the code into the keypad and left the room. Leaving the door open, he approached Sister Bernice, who was sitting at her desk in the hallway, reading her Bible. "Sister, please have maintenance replace the binding on Celeste's arms and legs. Double up on them and use the metal restraints this time."

The nun squinted. "What do you mean, Father? What's wrong with her bindings?"

The priest sighed. "The demon manifested itself and broke them. They need to be stronger, more secure."

"Yes, Father." Sister Bernice shot up from her chair and entered the room. Father MacLeod backtracked and peered inside. As he expected, the nun was inspecting Celeste, looking for signs of violation. Shaking his head, he started back to his office. There was no time to dwell on the sister's actions, he had a phone call to make, after which, he needed to clear his schedule for a trip to Goffstown.

THIRTEEN

Lynne lifted her glass and swished the scotch around a lone ice cube. The alcohol's peaty aroma tickled her nose, the liquid stinging as it passed through her throat. She had recognized it as top-shelf when Paul poured and, for a moment, her concern about her daughter receded as she admired his taste. Though it was a sipping scotch, she drained the glass in one long gulp. Placing it on the coffee table, she asked for another.

"You sure?" Paul asked.

"Yeah."

"Okay, but please, slow down." He leaned over on the couch and picked up the bottle of Talisker 18. He poured a small shot, pursed his lips, and handed it to her.

A smile conveyed her thanks. To demonstrate her appreciation, she took a small sip and placed the glass down.

Paul sat back and exhaled. "How are we going to handle this?"

After spending the morning at the hospital talking with the FBI, the local police, two physicians, and the staff psychologist, she and Paul had had enough. They informed them all that they were taking the children to Paul's home. The psychologist had hypothesized that their two children were confused, traumatized, their condition a coping mechanism. By switching identities, the girls could distance themselves from the incident—a way to project their fears outside of themselves. In familiar surroundings, the psychologist thought they would naturally revert to their former selves, eventually. Lynne jumped at the suggestion and consulted with Paul. They decided to work out more details after they arrived at his house.

The kids were now upstairs in Cindy's bedroom. A low thump above them had both eyeing the ceiling. "You think they're okay?" Lynne asked.

He smiled. "Yeah. There's no cracks, and I didn't hear anything break."

She reached for her scotch. "I'm not sure what to do next. If the psychologist is right, we should let them stay together for as long as possible so they can figure this out on their own."

"I've been thinking the same thing. Lynne, I don't know you all that well, hell, I barely know you at all, so forgive me if I'm out of place here. It seems the most prudent thing we could do is to let Lisa stay overnight with Cindy. Tomorrow, we could have Cindy spend the day at your home. Would you consider asking your husband or boyfriend to spend the evening here? I'd give you guys my bed, and I could sleep on the couch."

Lynne's face relaxed, her eyes softened. "Thank you. I was thinking the same thing, but I didn't know how to ask you without feeling awkward. I love the idea. However, I do need to let you know that I am a single mother, I don't have a boyfriend. I hope that's not a problem."

"It's not a problem for me. Did you bring Lisa up by yourself?"

She nodded. "Yes. I'm pretty much alone."

"No family?"

"I haven't spoken to my family since I was pregnant. I had an affair with an older man, a married man. My parents are born-again Christians, so, needless to say, it didn't go over too well with them."

"Oh, wow, I'm sorry. Did the father do anything to help you?"

Lynne nodded. "He reluctantly offered to take responsibility for the baby and support me as best he could as long as I didn't tell his wife. I accepted his offer. He wasn't wealthy, but between the contributions he made and my job, it was enough for us live comfortably."

"May I ask why you didn't seek child support through the courts?"

Lynne sighed. "It must be the scotch. I can't believe I'm telling you all of this."

"Oh, look, I didn't mean to pry or upset you. Forget I asked."

"No, it's okay. It feels good in a way to get it out, prevents me from being embarrassed later on if it comes up." She paused, then continued. "I didn't like the man. It started as a one-night stand, a decision made from loneliness and a bit too much alcohol. I had no intention of seeing him again. I did, though. It was exciting, and to be honest, the sex was good. After getting to know him better, I started falling for him. After a while, I came to the realization he was apathetic towards me so I thought it time to end the relationship before I became too invested." Lynne turned silent for a few seconds, and then shook her head. "Sure as hell, that's when I discovered I was pregnant. He demanded I abort the baby. I refused. We met a few more times after to talk it over, but he couldn't hide his resentment. Abuse followed, first verbal and then physical. I was afraid of him and decided I didn't want him involved in my life or my child's. He did keep his word on supporting Lisa, but the jerk died of a heart attack when she was three, and of course the money stopped."

Paul lifted his glass and downed his scotch. "Oh, man, I'm sorry that happened to you. Despite the lack of support after he died, it sounds like you have done all right by your daughter."

"I think so, too. What about you? From what I gather, you're single. What's your story?"

Reaching for the bottle, Paul poured himself a generous amount into his glass.

"Whoa," said Lynne, "you told *me* to go easy!"

Paul smiled, but she didn't think it sincere.

"Yeah. Talking about my wife isn't easy for me. This helps me numb the feelings."

"Oh, then maybe we should save it for another time."

"No, now's the right time. You shared your past. It's my turn. My wife was in an auto accident. She went through a stop sign and was hit by a tractor-trailer. She survived the impact but died later that night in the hospital. I won't go into the details, but when the investigation was finished, the police told me she was texting someone when the accident happened. When they gave me her phone along with the rest of her belongings, I went through it. I discovered she was having an affair."

"Oh my God! That must have been devastating! I'm so sorry."

Paul glazed over. "Thanks. It's been a couple of years now. I won't say I'm over it, but I have come to terms with it." He refocused his gaze on Lynne. "I'm not sure what hurt more, that I was not enough for her—that I was an inadequate husband—or that she had a side to her that I never knew."

Lynne straightened up. "What do you mean?"

"The man she was going to see wasn't the first time she cheated on me. There was evidence of others."

"Oh, no. Did you find out who she was seeing?"

"I called two numbers on her phone. Both ended up with recordings stating that the number was no longer in service. I'm guessing they used throwaway phones for the affairs."

"And she didn't?"

"No. Maybe she wanted me to find out."

Lynne asked, "Were there any names on the texts?"

"First names only."

After a short silence, Lynne spoke up. "I thought my story was bad, yours is so much worse. Where was Cindy when this happened?

"At daycare. My wife worked part time, in the mornings. She wanted the afternoons to herself to do errands, clean the house, and, I guess, to have affairs."

Another silence ensued; this time Paul broke it. "I hope you don't mind mac and cheese for dinner. It's one of Cindy's favorites."

Grateful for the change of subject, Lynne grinned. "Lisa's, too. But let me whip up something else for the two of us. I need to go to my apartment and get some things. I'll stop at the store on my way back and pick up some items. Pork chops okay?"

"I love pork chops. I'll take the kids out for a walk and..." Another thump on the ceiling cut him off. It was louder this time, with weight behind it. "We'd better go upstairs and see what they're doing." Hearing another thump, Paul chuckled. "I don't hear any crying, but yeah, let's go check it out now."

They climbed the stairs and stood before Cindy's closed bedroom door. They listened before entering and heard the two young girls giggling.

"Well, Paul, it doesn't sound like they're fighting, let's see what they're up to."

Paul let them into the room. When they passed the threshold, they both froze. The girls were three feet over the bed, suspended in mid-air. Upright and naked, they were pointing toward each other and chortling.

The girls' laughter stopped, and the blond girl's head spun toward Lynne. "Hey, Mommy, look what we can do."

There was no excitement in the girl's voice, no wonder. Her eyes were another matter. With a penetrating gaze, they bore into Lynne. She recognized the look—*defiance*. Numbness spread from her chest to the top of her head. She forced herself to break from the child's gaze and turned to Paul. He was facing her with his mouth open, shaking his head. A moment later, he turned back to the children and whispered, "Lynne, what the fuck is going on?"

FOURTEEN

Raised voices bounced off the walls of the stairway leading to their bedroom. Irene's husband stood at the bottom stair, listening. The words were muffled, as if spoken through a blown-out speaker, but there were no televisions or radios on the second floor. He had been inside the house for the past hour and no one had come in. Despite the poor sound quality, he knew one of those voices was hers. The other sounded like a man.

He stepped easy on the wooden treads. The voices grew louder, but still indistinct. At the top, he paused. His wife's voice was clearer now, but she wasn't speaking words. Moans filled his ears, and it didn't sound as if she were in pain.

She has a man in the bedroom with her.

His knees weakened at the thought, and he braced the wall to prevent himself collapsing. *How could she do this to me?* As the moans grew louder, shock gave way to anger. Who the hell could be in there with her? She had refused any kind of sex with him the past few months and now she was in bed with another man? This was getting to be too much, more than he could handle. *First she blows the newspaper guy, then she's covered in black jizz from that Dark Master demon she's always going on about.* His anger turned to rage. His muscles tightened, and his eyes burned with fury.

He rushed to their bedroom door but stopped short of grabbing the knob. While a part of him was afraid to have his suspicions confirmed, there was something else he was more scared of.

He was terrified of how his wife might react at the interruption.

There was no doubt she had become vindictive after those four men had taken her. It was all adding up. When she had instructed him to help kill those kids, it left no doubt her occult activities left little room for him in her life. He was being used, and he didn't like it. Add to that, she had never once informed him where his place would be once she had achieved her goals. He was coming to the conclusion there might not be one.

His hesitation dissolved when her moaning ceased. In its place, a screech so filled with pain his face tightened. His love for her overrode his doubt; he pulled the door open and rushed into the room.

He made it within four feet of the bed when he stopped cold. There was a brief outline of a man on his knees in front of Irene, but then he was gone. Donald looked around for him, but there was no one there. He focused his attention on Irene. She was sitting naked on the bed, her legs spread wide. Between them oozed a black fluid. It was not the sexual aspect of her position that froze him. Her body was in a state of flux. She went in and out of existence, slipping away like that man he thought he'd seen, and then returning. Her image flickered like old movie film that ran off the projection gears. Her facial features changed at the speed of a strobe light, morphing from ecstasy to outrage and madness. With his mouth open and his head shaking, Donald backed away from her. As he stared, her condition changed. The moments in which she was there increased, so he slowed his withdrawal. After a few more steps, he stopped. His wife had ceased flickering. She sat on the bed, solid now, her hands balled into fists and her face framed in a scowl.

"Fuck," she yelled, not bothering to acknowledge his presence, "who was that guy?"

Bewildered, he repeated her exclamation. "Fuck?" After a few seconds, he added, "You looked like someone kept switching you on and off, scaring me half to death, and the first thing you do is yell *fuck* and ask about some guy?"

"YES!"

He shrunk back as her anger grew.

"He was a fucking giant!" she screamed. "Where the hell did he come from? He ruined our plan!"

Donald didn't see any giant. The man between her legs appeared to be shorter than *he* was. This was an opening. "Irene, what the hell is this plan you're talking about? Where do I fit in?"

She swiveled her head toward him. Her eyes were as black as the fluid leaking from between her legs. The corners of her mouth lifted in a grin, but there was no happiness in that smile. "Come to me, Donald. I'll show you your place in my plans."

Irene lay back on the bed, her legs spread wide. The inky wetness bubbled, and small streams of black fluid dribbled down her thighs. Appalled, he cringed. *What has she become?* She implored him to come to her, to kneel between her knees, and she would share with him the wonder of the Dark Master. She repeated her request until it was all he could think of.

His resolve was weakening. After all, Irene was his wife, she loved him, and with all he had done for her, she would never hurt him. Lifting his eyes from her crotch to her face, he saw the woman he had married. She was beautiful, alluring. The calls to him continued, and he stepped toward her. Her voice was calm, soothing, and beckoning. His thoughts fogged over except for one—he needed her. He was erect, and the pressure to take her overwhelming. When he stood before her, he kneeled, eager to please. He leaned in, thirsty, ready to pleasure her, craving his own release. Closing his eyes, he opened his mouth, and his tongue brushed past his bottom lip.

When the odor hit him, he hesitated. Sulfur, pungent and bitter, stung his nose. It was as potent as a slap across the face. The fog in his head was lifting, his thoughts clearing. *What the fuck am I doing?* He pulled away.

Irene sat up and pulled him in to her. Combined with the suddenness of her action, her overpowering strength left no opportunity for resistance. His face collided with a wall of damp flesh. He was held against it with the pressure of a vice.

Donald couldn't breathe, couldn't scream. When the pain slammed into him, it was with the force of a hammer. Fire consumed his face, and his flesh burned. The nerve endings on the tip of his tongue exploded in agony before the ruined muscle slid down his chin. His nose and lips ignited and were seared to crusts. Skin sloughed from his forehead and cheeks, gathering as a pile at his neck where it amassed, cooled, and solidified. The muffled sounds of his struggle were lost as his ears dissolved in fiery anguish. Reflexes kicked in and he attempted to pull back, but she held him taut.

He tried to grab hold of her knees. He struggled and pushed, but her grip was secure. Moments later, his strength ebbed, and his attempt at freedom faltered. The muscles in his body slacked, and he went limp. Either as a result of shock or from the nerve damage in his face, the pain diminished.

One portion of his face had escaped the scalding; his eyes were untouched. Elsewhere, the pain had been intense, too severe to concentrate on his vision. Now that it receded, the view before him was clear. He was in one end of a tunnel, all sides consisting of tree husks. Clinging to the trees, thin tendrils of yellow smoke rose and danced along dead branches. At the end of the tunnel was the elongated face of a man. Its skin was dull and as black as the liquid that leaked from Irene. Wrinkled skin framed oval eyes the color of runny custard.

For the first time in his life, Donald wished he were dead.

"Donald," the face whispered, "we finally meet."

"No," he cried, "go away."

"Go away? We'll be spending much time together. I'm going to eat your soul, but not all at once. I'm going to save some for later."

As the face rushed toward him, Donald's wish was partially granted.

Irene released the pressure, and to her surprise, Donald was forcibly expelled from between her thighs. He didn't get far before gravity claimed his body. He crumpled to the floor, resting on his back, putting several feet between them. She was amused by the result. It was as if all the energy he had used to withdraw from her grip had been stored and ejected when she let him go. She decided that he resembled a damaged mannequin, a lifeless construct. The top and sides of his head were soaked with the Dark Master's inky fluid. What did Donald call that stuff when he discovered her covered in it? *Jizz.* He called it jizz. *Well, Donald, we were married, and you know how that saying goes...what's mine is yours.* Chuckling, she studied him further. All the skin from his face had been stripped. The bone gleamed as if acid-scrubbed and bleached.

Only the eyes remained untouched, sunken in their sockets, staring lifelessly at the ceiling.

"Donald, you wanted to know my plan, well, this has always been it," she said, gazing at his corpse. "You were so in love with me, I knew I could count on you. Did you know my kidnapping was part of the plan? I would guess not, as you were too stupid to figure it out—too gullible for your own good. Still, I could feel doubt take seed in your mind, so maybe you weren't that dumb after all. Now, what am I to do with you?"

Crippled as she was, his body was too heavy to drag downstairs, outside, and into the fields behind their barn. She would have to cut him into pieces, bag him, and make several trips to bury him. It would be messy and exhausting. If things had gone right with Manuel, she could have had him do it for her. Anger crept in as she recalled what had happened earlier. Whoever that giant man was, he was going to pay, and pay dearly. A consultation with the Dark Master was in order, and she would appeal to him for guidance on how to handle the brute after she finished burying her husband.

She stood from the bed to go down to the cellar for the proper tools. At the bedroom door, she paused to figure out what she needed, and took a final look at what was left of her husband. Donald's eyes swiveled from the ceiling toward her. She yelped and stepped back. After she collected herself, she said, "Dismembering you is going to be interesting, Donald."

FIFTEEN

The pawnshop owner kicked aside a number of splintered two-by-fours and ragged sections of plywood littering the floor. Eyeing his work, he bent over and ran his hand over the fully exposed shew-stone. Formed as a loose oval-like structure, the object was the size of an oven. Sculpted from marble, the gray and white striations were distinct, though dulled with age. The majority of the surface was uneven, rough to the touch, indicating the stone might not have been fully polished when the sculpture was completed. Further to this line of reasoning, pick marks and punch divots were scattered throughout, with one crevice exceptionally deep— possibly the work of an axe. The exception to all this wear was a circle approximately a foot in diameter. It was on the side, facing the entrance of the pawnshop. Its composition was a mystery. The circle was as dark and dull as a forgotten piece of coal in the corner of a cellar, but the surface was smooth as sea glass. He seemed to recall that volcanic glass was often used in the sixteenth century for reflective surfaces, and made a mental note to look it up.

It wasn't normal for the proprietor to examine goods if the customer deemed them authentic and payment was forwarded before receipt. While the majority of his business was comprised of researching and then procuring esoteric items for interested parties, he occasionally accepted clients who asked him to hold merchandise for pickup. All customers required anonymity when purchasing goods or using his shop as a temporary storage area—they knew they could trust him to ensure their confidentiality. For his part, the proprietor secured a hefty commission, occasionally while doing little work. It was supposed to be the case with this shew-stone, but it was proving to be anything but a normal transaction.

Earlier that afternoon, an email arrived in his business account. The sender informed him that the customer who had purchased the stone was recently deceased and would not be taking possession of the object. They went on to say the customer's business associates had been unaware of this purchase. After researching the details of the transaction, they had attempted to trace the origin of the purchase to return it for a refund. Unable to find the seller, they decided to write off the purchase. The pawnshop owner was to keep all monies paid and retain ownership of the object.

Intrigued and suspicious, the pawnshop owner called the phone number supplied by the original customer. Though their conversations had been limited, he had had no trouble reaching the man when needed. After punching the numbers in, he heard a click, then silence. *Perhaps the message is being recorded, an automatic trace placed on the caller.* Though he had no worries about the call being traced back to him, he hung up quickly. No sense in taking unnecessary risks.

After giving the matter some thought, he had decided not to respond to the email. When he went to save it to a folder, there was another unusual occurrence—the correspondence had disappeared. Having no idea if an email could self-delete, he frowned. He closed the laptop, placed it under the counter.

Entering the residential portion of the building through a well-disguised steel door at the rear of the pawnshop, he returned a few minutes later with a hammer and crowbar.

Now, bent over with scraps of lumber scattered around the stone, his fingers ran over the surface of the circle. *Does this thing work?* All his years running the pawnshop had proven anything was possible, so he closed his eyes and concentrated on the tips of his fingers.

Nothing came to him.

He decided to approach it another way. He might gain access if he addressed it directly. With nothing to lose except for feeling a bit foolish, he decided to go for broke. He leaned in closer to the mirrored surface and whispered, "Who is behind the recent attack on the pawnshop?"

If the stone was clairvoyant, it wasn't giving up its secrets. Taking a deep breath, he straightened up and cast a wary eye on the object. Either the man who had purchased this object was taken for an expensive ride, or a key of some sort was needed to unlock its abilities. *I need to research John Dee and find out*—a thump at the front of the shop diverted his attention.

The doors rattled for a few moments, then the pawnshop owner heard a key being inserted into the lock. Beside himself, only one other person possessed a key.

Rex.

The shop doors swung open. The giant stood in the opening, blocking out much of the afternoon sunlight. While Rex had worked there for a little over a year, he had nowhere near the experience the proprietor had when dealing with the strange occurrences associated with the shop. He did, however, have enough experience to exercise caution. Rex surveyed the area. When satisfied there were no threats, he stepped through the doorway, but halted after a few feet. From behind him, an older man stepped to Rex's side. He wore a deer-in-headlights expression—a look the pawnshop owner had seen many a time on those who had the misfortune of meeting Rex. For many of them, it would be their last pain-free moment. The giant closed the doors to the shop, pointed at the proprietor, and motioned for his companion to approach.

"Hello," the older man offered, taking tentative steps forward. "My name is Manuel."

Manuel's eyes darted around the shop and his hands were shaking. Facial features and skin tone indicated Spanish or Latin descent, his name reinforcing that notion. If pressed, he would have guessed the man was in his late fifties. The visitor's unkempt hair and wrinkled clothes suggested that he hadn't bathed in days. After the incident with the possessed woman, the pawnshop owner was wary of any strangers entering the shop. Rex would have known that. If his assistant had brought this man here in one piece, there had to be a good reason. Lately, Rex had not exhibited any signs of the madness he suffered occasionally, and the pawnshop owner had been comfortable around him since the incident with the possessed woman. He would give the pair a chance to explain, but first, he would attempt to put the visitor at ease. A confrontation, or tepid response, which would normally be his initial reaction, would have the opposite effect. This man was timid, scared, and would need some reassuring before opening up. With a light tone, he asked, "What brings you to my establishment, Manuel?"

The man's facial expression was not one the proprietor was expecting; he was clearly anguished. His shoulders dipped, he bit his lower lip, and closed his eyes tight. A tear clung to the bridge of his nose. Recognizing the signs of a man suffering from the pressures of a heavy burden, the pawnshop owner let his guard down, but only a little. It came to him that Rex had one more soft spot, other than abused animals and helpless women. What was it in this man that had touched his assistant with pity? It was an unusual occurrence for Rex, and the proprietor's curiosity was piqued. While the older man may have exposed a crack in his emotional façade, he wasn't entirely broken. After composing himself, he gave an answer.

"I—I don't know. This guy," he said, pointing to Rex, "saved my life and then asked me to come along and meet you." The words came faster. "Mister, I don't know you, and I've lived here forever, it seems, but I've never seen this pawnshop before, and so much has happened to me, and I think Irene is working with some kind of demon—"

"Whoa, slow down!" The pawnshop owner led the man to the counter, and then walked to the other side. Rex remained on the outside and positioned himself behind Manuel. The proprietor reached under the counter and removed a notebook and a pencil, placing it between them. "Okay, Manuel, start from the beginning."

Manuel told the man behind the counter everything, starting from when he first saw Duck Lady walking by his office to Rex pulling him away from her in his house. Initially, his story came out in a jumbled rush, but after he was admonished to slow down several times, he was able to get it out coherently. As the details poured out of him, he alternated between bouts of relief that someone was not only listening to him but not passing judgment, to mind-numbing horror as he relived the details.

He assumed the man behind the counter was the owner of the pawnshop. At one point, he asked the man his name but was rebuffed, which made him feel somewhat slighted. He got over it quickly as he resumed his story. As Manuel related what had happened to him, the owner wrote in his notebook, jotting down key words and phrases rather than whole sentences. When the tale ended with his walking into the pawnshop with Rex, the proprietor closed the notebook and stashed it under the counter.

"Okay, Manuel, I have several questions to ask you. I hope you don't mind."

"No, I don't. I'll do anything to figure out how to deal with this mess. I asked you your name earlier and you didn't answer. I'd like to know the name of the man I'm talking to."

The pawnshop owner set a steely gaze on him. "You said you are a reporter, I'm telling you right now that none of what we discuss goes into the newspaper. Not a single quote, not the content of the discussion, not a word about the pawnshop, and especially no mention of me or Rex."

Manuel nodded. "It won't, I promise. I just want this to end."

The pawnshop owner sighed. "If you feel you have to address me personally, call me, ahhh, call me Mr. Jones."

"Thank you, Mr. Jones—I—"

The doors of the pawnshop slammed open. When they hit the wall, Manuel jumped. Neither Mr. Jones nor Rex reacted to the noise other than to turn their heads to the sound.

The doorway was empty.

After a few moments' silence, Manuel faced the pawnshop owner. The man's eyes continued to focus on the empty space. Manuel swung his gaze back to the doors. His shoulders jerked.

A young blond-haired girl stood at the threshold. She couldn't have been more than eight or nine, skinny, with long, thin hair curling up at her shoulders. When she stepped over the threshold, none of them moved or called to her. The proprietor asked Rex if he had locked the doors after he ushered Manuel in. Rex grunted in the affirmative.

Manuel studied the young girl. She was *off,* somehow. Childish innocence was absent from her eyes. They were fierce, determined. Entering further, her gait lacked the usual hesitancy that you might expect from someone of her age. Her steps were measured, made with purpose. Manuel thought her expressionless, with lips tight and straight. Adding to the oddness of the situation, she remained silent as she progressed into the pawnshop, taking in her surroundings.

The owner, who remained behind the counter, was the first to address her. He did not speak to her as one would a child. The question he asked was loud and direct. "Can I help you, young lady?"

If she had heard the question, she refused to acknowledge it, but she did change her path to the direction of the counter. Manuel gasped and stepped back as she made her next move.

The child jumped onto the countertop.

The counter had to be at least four feet up from the floor. It would take an athlete to accomplish the task. This little girl couldn't have weighed more than 50 pounds. The jump itself appeared to take little effort, it was as if she floated up, guided by unseen hands. Not once did she gaze at her feet or her target. There was no clump when her shoes hit the worn hardwood. No balancing act or deep breath when she landed.

Manuel observed the pawnshop owner. The man displayed no reaction to the child's leap. He remained in place, watching the girl, waiting for an answer. Rex, on the other hand, stiffened, his hands curled into fists.

The child stepped up to the pawnshop owner. She set her sight on him, staring. After a few moments, she smiled. "You have something in here we want."

The proprietor flinched. "Might I have your name?"

A giggle emerged. "You know better than to ask me that. But if you need to address me, you can call me Lisa, but I used to be called Cindy."

"Tell me, Lisa," the pawnshop owner responded, "What is it I have that you are in need of?"

"Oh, you know." The child winked.

"Suppose you humor me."

Eyes narrowed, Lisa leaned into the man. "The Prexy Box, you fool. Give us the Prexy Box."

The pawnshop owner closed the gap between them to a few inches. "No."

"CINDY! ... I mean *Lisa!*"

The call came from the front door of the pawnshop. All four of them turned to the source. A man hurried toward them, with another young girl in tow. When he arrived at the counter, he lifted the child off the counter. "I—I'm so sorry, gentlemen. I was out walking with my daughter and her friend and somehow, Lisa got away from me. We looked everywhere for her. Thank God she's all right. After everything I've been through—"

Manuel interrupted him. "You're the man whose daughter was abducted. Paul. You might not remember, but we've met a number of times. Look, there's something wrong here—"

Paul's demeanor went from that of a concerned father to one of suspicion. "Yes, I remember. I also remember reading that you are supposed to be in jail. They think you kidnapped Cindy and those other kids."

"No, I had nothing to do with it. They released me on bail after new evidence came in. The police chief believes I'm innocent."

Paul shook his head. "Man, I don't know what to believe anymore. I don't know what to think. So much crazy shit has happened. You said 'there's something wrong here'. What did you mean?"

Manuel noticed the two children hanging on to Paul. They clung to his legs as if they were afraid, but their expressions betrayed something else. Each had one eye closed. A sign of defiance? A signal of threat? Maybe both. "Paul, is there a time we can talk when the children aren't around? If you are nervous about me, maybe we can meet back here with Mr. Jones later on and discuss it. It's important we talk." The pawnshop owner nodded in agreement.

Paul eyed the giant standing at the counter.

The proprietor spoke up. "His name is Rex. His presence will be required when we talk. He won't hurt you, unless you give him a reason to."

Shaking his head, Paul said, "I don't know. So much has happened, and now this. All I was doing was taking the kids for a walk while Lisa's mother gathered some groceries. What the hell is all this about? Why should I come back and talk to you?"

The pawnshop owner pointed to the blond-haired child. "That is not your daughter."

Visibly nervous, Paul shook. "How—how do you know that?" Hesitating a moment, he patted the young African-American girl on the head. "For the love of God, I don't know how, but *this* is my daughter."

"Please explain," asked the proprietor.

Manuel could see the reluctance on Paul's face. Despite this, Paul launched into his story. As it poured out of him, Paul started to look relieved. As a journalist, he had seen this before. If someone was carrying a heavy load and had a chance to vent, they couldn't help themselves from divulging all they knew. Hell, he'd been through the same thing with the pawnshop owner earlier. When Paul finished, it was as if Manuel absorbed the man's fear.

After a moment, the pawnshop owner pointed to the African-American child. "She is not your daughter, either."

Paul stiffened. A loud sigh escaped his chest before he spoke. "I'm scared to death by what that means, but I have to know. Can I come back later this evening? Around nine o'clock?"

The pawnshop owner answered for Manuel and Rex. "Yes."

Upset, but managing to control it, Paul led the children to the front doors. Someone outside the shop diverted his attention. He nodded a greeting and left, girls in tow. Seconds later, that person walked into the shop. The man's white collar announced his profession—a priest. He surveyed the shop, and his gaze fell on the owner. His voice light, he said, "You don't make it easy to find you."

The pawnshop owner stared hard at the man. After a few uncomfortable moments of silence, he replied, his answer not reflecting the jovial mood of his guest. "We move around a lot."

If his tone bothered the priest, he didn't let it show. He closed the double doors, and then advanced toward the three men. "Rex! How you doing? Kill anyone lately?"

Rex didn't miss a beat. "Not today." Giving the priest a glance from head to toe, he added, "But it's still early."

Once again, their new guest shook off the sentiment. He extended a hand to Manuel. "I'm Father MacLeod, nice to meet you. And you are?"

"My name is Manuel Chance. I take it you are a friend of Mr. Jones?"

Eyebrows knitted, the priest said, "Mr. Jones?"

"Yes." Manuel pointed to the pawnshop owner.

A hearty laugh erupted from the priest. "Mr. Jones, huh? What happened to Mr. Smith? You are an enigma."

The pawnshop owner didn't miss a beat. "What brings you to my establishment, Father MacLeod?"

Any amusement the priest was harboring vanished. "We need to talk."

"Does this concern Celeste?"

"Yes and no. The demon continues to reside in Celeste. It has made contact with me. Like I said, we need to talk."

At the mention of a demon, Manuel's chest tightened. He wondered what the hell was going on.

"Rex," directed the proprietor, "escort Manuel to one of the guest rooms. He will be staying with us for a while. Please watch over him. I'd like you both to come back at nine o'clock, for our meeting with Paul. In the meantime, if you need me, I will be here with Father MacLeod."

As Manuel followed Rex through the disguised steel door in the pawnshop, he glanced over his shoulder. The priest waved to him. Manuel shuddered as the door closed behind him.

"Before we begin, take off your collar and unbutton your shirt," the pawnshop owner demanded of the priest.

MacLeod chuckled. "After all we've been through? I thought you had the hots for Celeste, not me."

Though crudely stated, there was truth in the priest's comment.

"Quit stalling."

"You still don't trust me?"

"No."

The last time the two had met, MacLeod had possession of a trinket in the care of the pawnshop owner—a necklace he entrusted to Celeste. The necklace had belonged to a sixth-century monk and purported to be imbued with an ability to prevent the wearer's body from decomposing after death. As they had learned with the events at the Moore House, it also had powers to *protect* the wearer from a supernatural death. Celeste had been wearing the necklace when the demon James Moore possessed her, and, though she was still alive, she was in a comatose state. The pawnshop owner had asked MacLeod to return the necklace, but was told it was now in the possession of the Catholic Church. He didn't believe it. If the priest still had the necklace, he would be smart enough not to wear it to the pawnshop. By calling the priest out on it, the pawnshop owner was asserting his rightful ownership.

MacLeod pulled the lapels of his suit coat aside, removed his collar, and unfastened the top three buttons on his white shirt. "Satisfied?"

"No, not really."

The two of them held eye contact. The pawnshop owner didn't want to show weakness, and he assumed the priest felt the same. It was MacLeod who flinched first. He placed his collar into his suit coat pocket and fastened his shirt back up, leaving the top button open. "Any other requests before we get serious?"

Sighing, the pawnshop owner shook his head. "No. Okay, why are you here?"

The priest proceeded to walk around the shop. "You know, it's been a while since I've been inside here. I did come to visit you after we concluded the Moore House exorcism, but you were closed. Funny thing, though, I could have sworn you were located on the far side of the main street."

"As I said, we move around a lot."

"The whole building?" When he didn't receive an answer, he walked toward the large stone against the far wall. As he rubbed the smooth circle on its surface, he asked, "This is interesting, what does it do? Grant wishes? Detect evil? Forecast the weather?"

"It's supposed to be a shew-stone, a divining mirror. It came my way through an unorthodox manner, and I haven't had the time to research it."

"A shew-stone? The only reference I know of a shew-stone is one from the late sixteenth century. John Dee, as I recall, and that one was called a scrying stone. That relic is supposed to be housed in England."

The pawnshop owner was impressed; he softened his tone. "Yeah, I know. This is said to be Dee's scrying stone, so either this one is a fake or the one in the British Museum is. Seems there isn't much information available to the public."

"I have some contacts that may be useful. I'll work on it when I have some time."

The owner was unsure how to interpret the offer. As long as the stone resided in the pawnshop, it would be almost impossible for it to be removed by human intervention. If the priest was looking to benefit from the research, there was little he could do with it.

"That's settled then. Mr. ...ugh...Smith, or Jones, or whatever the hell you are calling yourself today, we have some serious business to discuss."

The pawnshop owner shook his head. "You know, I'm sure whatever you want to talk about is important, but I've got enough on my plate right now. Even if it involves Celeste, I can't take the time to help her at this moment."

Father MacLeod stepped away from the stone. "Even if it involves the Prexy Box?"

That got his attention. "What do you know about the Prexy Box?"

"Other than it could lead to the destruction of the world, not much. I suggest we exchange information."

The pawnshop owner walked to the front of the shop and locked the doors. Remaining silent, he unfolded a pair of metal chairs he kept against the wall and placed them in front of the counter. "You first." Sitting, they began a conversation that would last an hour.

"As I understand this," the pawnshop owner began, "two demons, one of whom is Lucifer, who is the good guy in your story, are at war with each other. The other demon, the bad demon, whose name we don't know other than the Dark Master, wants the Prexy Box so he can release the souls it has imprisoned so he would have an army to take control over the world. Your God is watching all of this, and if he decides he doesn't like the outcome, He'll also destroy the world. Am I correct so far?"

Father MacLeod nodded.

"Okay. Another demon, James Moore, one that tried to kill us all, comes and relates all this to you and explains a way to avoid certain catastrophe. The solution involves you taking possession of the Prexy Box before the bad guy does, and then following some mysterious instructions. Have I got that right?"

"Yeah, you got that right. You know, Mr. Smith, sorry, I can't seem to think of you with any other name, you catch on fast."

The pawnshop owner's forehead wrinkled. "You're leaving something out. Why would James Moore come to you? Why would you agree to assist him? You don't strike me as the do-gooder type."

Hurt flashed over the priest's face. "You cut me deep, Mr. Smith. I find it fascinating that you listen to this fantastic tale and, at its conclusion, you don't question one bit of it. Instead, you accuse me of not being forthright."

"Cut the crap. What are you holding back?"

The priest sighed. "Yeah, you're right. I made a deal with a demon years ago to save my nephew's life. I still owe on that deal. If I assist James Moore in this, not only do I save the world, my side of the bargain will be considered fulfilled."

"If the world were to end, either by God's hand or the demon's control over it, why would you care about your bargain? It seems there would be no reason to fulfill it."

"Ah," replied MacLeod, "there's the rub. First, I don't want the world to end. I rather enjoy living. Second, we know there's an afterlife. Shit, we're talking about demons, for fuck's sake, not to mention God destroying the world because no one would be around to make Him feel relevant. We've both seen the worst of the afterlife. If it's possible, I'd rather avoid spending eternity suffering in it because I tried to save my nephew's life. So, let's say all this is true, if we do what we are asked to, we will be the superheroes who saved the world. I think it would win me favor with the big guy up there."

"So, really, this *is* all about you."

"Mr. Smith, I've told my side of the story, now it's your turn. I want to know everything."

The proprietor started with the story of a possessed woman driving halfway across the country to die in his shop and ended with the little girl who had supernatural jumping abilities. "So, priest, that's where we're at. We are all meeting here at nine o'clock tonight. You should join us."

The priest shook his head. "Come on, you mean I'm going to have to tell this all over again? Shit. Can't you just give me this Prexy Box and I'll go on my way saving the world?"

The pawnshop owner didn't bother replying.

Father MacLeod threw his hands up. "All right, I'll be back here at nine. I'm pretty sure I can find a way to pass the next few hours."

The proprietor led the priest to the door and unlocked it. After MacLeod had been gone for a few minutes, he walked behind the counter and pressed some keys on his computer. He had recorded their conversation; it warranted another listen.

SIXTEEN

Irene sat at the dinner table; her dress left a watery trail from the front door to her seat. She had hosed off the blood, chunks of gristle, bone, and dirt that she had accumulated dismembering her husband. Cutting him into pieces hadn't been easy, but she was determined to finish it up quickly. Though her disfigurement was a hindrance, she had delighted in the task. The smile never left her face as she took her time washing off the remains of her husband, replaying the killing scene in her mind as she scrubbed.

She had started with Donald's head; she'd figured it would be easier to start at the top and work her way down. He was on his back, so she lifted his upper body and placed a large pillow between his shoulder blades. This allowed his head to tilt back, exposing the neck. When the skin had melted from his face, this was where it settled, clinging to his neck like a tumor. After she placed the bone saw on his throat and rested it there, she noticed movement.

His eyes darted from left to right, taking her in. Somehow they had been spared. With the flesh burned off his skull, they were the only features remaining. Rolled up to his forehead when she had entered the room, now they stared at her, following her movements. Amused, she thought with his nose gone, he should have an unobstructed view as she cut him to pieces. She giggled at the thought, but her next one sobered her. Was he really dead? A quick check of his vital signs—a feel on his wrist for a pulse, her hand on his chest to check for breathing, and a placement of her cheek close to his mouth—confirmed he was lifeless.

Curiosity got the best of her.

"Donald, I know your ears are gone, but let me know, can you hear me? If so, look up and then down."

Her husband's eyes shot to the top of their sockets and then back down. Irene was euphoric.

"Well, Donald, it appears you are dead, but somehow, your thought process is still functioning inside that skull of yours. Let's see how active it is."

She drew the saw blade across his neck.

There was no sign of pain.

As the blade ripped his flesh, blood appeared at the wound, but there were no red drips, no gushing of fluid—another sign his heart wasn't pumping. Shifting her weight for leverage, she placed one hand against his forehead, working the saw with the other hand. Though it was designed for animal slaughter, sawing though his neck bones took effort.

Finished, Irene dropped the saw, and stood back to admire her handiwork. Leaning down, Irene placed her two bloody hands on the sides of Donald's skull. Lifting it up, they stared at each other. "I have just the place for you," she said, and placed his head on the bureau, facing his body. Bloody prints on each side of his skull contrasted against the white bone. "You can watch me while I work," she said, and resumed her task.

Once she had finished dicing him up into manageable pieces, she placed the body parts in plastic bags and cardboard boxes, lugging them out to the field by the shack where Donald had held the kidnapped children. She didn't bother burying them; the abundance of coyotes and bobcats would make short work of the remains. The Dark Master would ensure it. After cleaning up the mess in the bedroom, she burned all the rags, scatter rugs, and soiled sheets in the stove in the barn. It was hard work, took hours, and at the finish, the hose removed as much sweat from her body as it did her husband's bits and fluids.

Now, sitting at the dining room table, she peered at the opposite end where Donald usually sat. Of course, the chair was empty. She had to acknowledge there was a small corner of her heart that would miss him. He was simple but devoted, and the house would be that much quieter from hereon in. It was a pragmatic thought, no hint of remorse underlying it. Recalling that his head was upstairs, gathering dust on the nightstand, it occurred to her that he might still be around for a while. Unable to speak, he wouldn't be the best company, but apparently, he could still hear her. It would be nice to have someone to talk to, at least until the Dark Master's plans came to fruition and she was standing by his side. With the thought of his promised power, she rose from the chair and proceeded to the bedroom.

Standing on the same spot where she had dismembered her husband, Irene removed her wet clothes except for her panties, and tossed them into a pile. Once fully naked, she stepped over to the nightstand and cleaned off Donald's head with her underwear, adjusting it so he would have a direct view of their bed. His eyes tracked her as she stepped away. She lay down on the mattress. Spreading her legs wide, she invoked the demon. Her hands caressed her breasts and the tattoos on her body went into motion. Symbols shifted positions. Inked silhouettes of the grotesque slithered and twisted around her torso and extremities. She thrust her pelvis up and closed her eyes. An offering.

Irene's wait for her lover wasn't long.

The demon floated inches above her.

As it penetrated her, her ass sunk deep into the mattress. Opening her eyes, she saw the Dark Master's face. The yellow in its eyes gleamed, and its smile was immense. *He's enjoying this as much as I am.* Despite its length and girth, she felt no pain, following each of its thrusts with one of her own. *Donald, I hope you are seeing this.*

The demon grabbed her asscheeks and gave her one final push. Its fluids drained into her and she climaxed. Pleasure coursed through her pelvis as an image of black semen filling her and overflowing ran through her mind.

Releasing her after it was spent, the Dark Master pushed back and knelt before her spread legs. "You called for me, Irene."

"Yes. I need to talk to you."

Her lover's eyes bored into hers. "We *do* have much to discuss."

Irene blinked. Its tone was harsh, condescending—not what she was expecting.

"Master, I—I wanted to ask you when I will be standing by your side. We've come so far in the past few months. I've done everything you've asked. I need more power in order to continue to serve you. There is no beauty in my body. It is weak. If I am to further serve your path to return, I need strength. I need more ability to control others."

The demon leaned forward. "My own strength is limited, woman. I need numbers. My return rests on having more of my own kind to stand with me, to worship me, to provide me with sustenance. My army resides in that box. You chose me, woman. You called to me all those months ago with a promise to assist me. Your efforts are failing. I've given you abilities no human has had before and you have squandered them. Your plan for the newspaperman collapsed before it started. Not only has he spurned you, he has joined forces with others and is now a threat."

Anger replaced Irene's fear. "Wait, I had Manuel! He was mine! Who was that giant that came and pulled him away? You should have seen him coming! How the hell did he pop up out of nowhere?"

Irene regretted the outburst immediately. The last thing she wanted to do was to piss this demon off. "I—I'm sorry," she offered. "The thing is, Manuel slipped from my hands, and I still don't understand how."

The demon glared at Irene but remained silent. After several seconds, it leaned back and addressed her. "The giant is working with the pawnshop owner. I do not know why he was at the journalist's home. I will work on removing him." The demon raised his arm and pointed at her.

An unseen hand pressed into Irene's back. There was a sensation of pressure against her hump, and she pushed back against it. There was pain, but she tolerated it. Soon, the pressure vanished, as did the pain. She slid off the bed and stood upright for the first time in months. She stepped to the mirror and angled her body so she could see her back. It was flat, lean, and the tattoos showed no sign of distortion. She faced the demon with her head bowed. "Thank you."

The demon swung his legs over the bed and stood before her. "I will send one of my underlings to the pawnshop for another attempt to seize the box. If he is unsuccessful, he will at least wear them down, make it easier for you if you are needed. I expect the giant will be there; if so, he will be addressed."

"Why don't you go to the pawnshop yourself?"

"You dare question me?" The demon's eyes blazed. "You are my surrogate! I am in you! I work through you!" It leaned toward her. "I cannot physically manifest unless I am called, either as you have done, or if someone summons me by name. When I am called by my name, the other might know of my location. That cannot happen until I have my army."

Puzzled, she asked, "You're afraid of God?"

The demon turned away from her. "Right now, He is the least of my worries."

"I don't understand. Who frightens *you*?"

It restored eye contact with her and stared until she looked away in fear. "Do as I say, woman. Do not fail me again."

Staring back into his yellow eyes, she answered. "I won't."

SEVENTEEN

"I want to be at that meeting, Paul," Lynne demanded.

"Yeah, but there's a problem. Who's going to watch the kids?"

After Paul returned from the pawnshop, he had sent the two girls upstairs to play so he could have a discussion with Lynne. She was placing the pork chops in the oven when he walked into the kitchen. Her smile vanished when she saw the expression on his face. Lynne stood still as he recounted the discussion at the pawnshop.

Lynne sighed. "Do you know anybody we could ask to watch them?"

"I could ask Tom and Sheila. The thing is, I'm going to have to tell them what's been going on. Hell, I don't know if they'll even believe me. Worse, what if they do agree, and the kids start floating in the air in front of them?"

"We can talk to the children before we go. Tell them not to do that or display any other weird talent they might discover."

Paul hung his head. "They're still kids, Lynne. They could promise anything in the moment and then forget."

Lynne walked to him and lifted his chin. "We'll promise them something, give them an incentive to be good. Look, this is a chance for me to find out what the hell is going on. Lisa, as much as Cindy, is a part in all this craziness. I need to be at that meeting with you."

"Okay, I'll ask Tom and Sheila. They'll think we're nuts. We're going to have to convince them that the girls are dealing with their kidnapping trauma by pretending to be each other. Let's not say anything about the kids floating, it might be a little too much for them to process."

Sheila heard the distress in Paul's voice. She wasted no time gathering Tom from his tinkering in the garage. "He wants us to look after the kids this evening," she told her husband, "but first, he wants us to come over, now. Said he has to tell us something important."

They wasted no time heading to Paul's.

As Paul and Lynne explained what had transpired since they were reunited with their children, Sheila sat motionless, unsure how to respond. This had to be a prank, but their inflections and expressions didn't reflect humor. If anything, both their faces exhibited a mixture of confusion and sadness. What she didn't detect was fear, which she took as a sign that they might be messing with her and Tom.

When Paul and Lynne finished their story, Sheila let out a nervous laugh. "If you two are messing with us, I have to say, you guys are doing a good job."

Lynne spoke first. "We're not making this up, Sheila. All of this really happened."

"Yes," echoed Paul, "it really did."

Tom finally commented. "Can we see the kids?"

Paul rose from his chair, went to the stairs, and called them down.

After an awkward greeting, Sheila and Tom peppered the kids with questions. When the children had had enough and their attentions veered from the conversation, Paul allowed them to go back to their rooms.

Sheila looked Paul in his eyes and shook her head. "That was so weird. They appear to genuinely believe who they say they are. Haven't they noticed their skin colors are different?"

"No," Paul replied.

"I'm sure you've brought them to psychologists. What did they say?"

"They're the ones who told us the trauma of being kidnapped is responsible for this, and over time, they will realize who they are."

Sheila lowered her gaze. "I'm so sorry you guys are going through this. How are you going to deal with it? I mean, how do you decide which child is yours?"

"We're still trying to work all that out. We're going to see someone this evening who may give us some insight into all of this. We would appreciate it if you could watch them so Paul and I can both make the meeting."

Tom jumped in. "Of course we will. What time do you want us here?"

Lynne replied, "Eight-thirty would be great. They will be in bed by then, so I don't think you'll have any issues with them."

"We'll be here," said Sheila.

Paul added, "If things get weird, you have my number. Don't hesitate to call."

Sheila made herself comfortable on the couch while Tom claimed the recliner. True to Paul and Lynne's word, the kids were upstairs in bed when they arrived. In the last hour, she hadn't heard so much as a thump from upstairs. Tom was engrossed in a Tom Piccirilli novel, and she was deep into

Hannahwhere by John McIlveen. They had decided earlier that they would keep the television off—better to hear the kids if there was a problem.

Developing a thirst, Sheila used the back flap of the novel as a bookmark and closed the book. "Tom, you want anything?"

Sheila froze. Both of the girls were standing behind the recliner. The girl she thought of as Cindy was staring at the back of Tom's head, and the other girl was staring at her.

Holding her shock in check, Sheila asked her husband to turn around. He slipped a ribbon into his book, closed it, and faced her. The worried expression on her face caused him to swivel around to see behind him. He jumped when he made eye contact with the girls.

He stood up, his heart racing. "Holy shit, you girls scared the hell out of me."

Both girls broke off their stares and giggled. In unison, they said, "We were trying to scare you."

Tom took a deep breath, stared at the ceiling for a few seconds, and then addressed them. "You know, that's not nice. I was scared, and I don't like that. How did you girls get down here without us hearing you?"

The blond-haired girl answered. "My name is Lisa. You don't know me, but I'm a friend of Cindy's." The other girl beamed when the name was mentioned. "We're sorry. We thought it would be fun."

Sheila didn't think the young girl was sorry at all. A crooked smile adorned her face, but her eyes were hard.

"Why are you girls up?" Sheila asked. "You were in bed when we came over."

The girl who now called herself Cindy spoke up. "We want to tell you a story, Mrs. White. I have one for you, and Lisa has one for Mr. White."

Sheila shook her head. "I don't know, girls, it's awfully late. Can't you read a story upstairs in your beds?"

The blond girl replied. "No, we don't want to read a story, we want to tell *you* a story. We have one for both of you."

"Sheila," Tom said, "let them tell us their stories. After that, we can send them back to bed."

"I have a bad feeling about this," whispered Sheila. Seeing first-hand how the two girls thought they were each other was more unnerving than she'd expected. The way they were acting, coming downstairs without making a sound, staring at her and Tom, and that giggle. The creepiness of the situation now outweighed her curiosity. Uneasiness rooted itself in her mind. *Say no. Just tell them to go to bed.*

Sheila heard a single word, spoken sternly, loudly. *"No!"*

She wondered if the reply was imagined—a result of her apprehension about the girls. Tom didn't react if he heard it; he was talking to the blond-haired girl in hushed tones. The girl on his lap replied, but the words were barely audible. Sheila strained to hear their conversation, but the other girl distracted her as she wormed her way onto Sheila's lap.

"You know I'm Cindy, right?"

Sheila didn't reply.

"Well, I am. I know I look different, but that's a mistake."

"A mistake?"

"Yeah, but it's not important, just an inconvenience."

Sheila was going to ask where the girl had learned the word "inconvenience", but didn't have the chance.

"I'm going to tell you a story—well, it's not really a story, it's the truth. I need you to close your eyes while I tell it. You need to listen carefully, hear every word I say. I want you to picture the story as I'm telling it."

The child's voice was soft, reassuring, the cadence slow. Sheila's mind felt cloudy, like it did after reading a book late into the night. She blinked a few times. She closed her eyes. Cindy's voice was clear, as if she were whispering in her ear.

"Did you know that Paul likes you?"

"Yes," Sheila murmured, "he's a nice man."

"Well, Paul *really* likes you. He thinks about you all the time. He thinks you are very attractive. Sexy. Did you know he stares at you when your back is turned? He does, you know. You know something else?"

Sheila knew this was wrong, but part of her wanted to hear this.

"Yes, I'd like to know more."

"Well, at night, I hear him. He calls your name. Sometimes he whispers it. Sometimes he shouts it. My dad wants you, maybe he even loves you."

Sheila sighed. Warmth spread through her lower body.

"He wouldn't be able to tell you," Cindy continued, "you're married. But, I know that if you made yourself available to Paul, he would take you."

A groan, filled with the promise of pleasure, escaped Sheila's lips.

"You need to sleep now and dream of what Paul could do to you. When you wake up, those dreams will stay with you. When the opportunity comes, you should act on those dreams. He wants it. Do you?"

"Yes."

Before Sheila's vision darkened, she turned to Tom. His eyes were closed as he leaned back on the recliner. The blond-haired girl was whispering in his ear.

Cindy stood alongside Lisa at the center of the living room. Sheila was fast asleep on her side. With a blanket covering her, she took up the entire couch with one hand snuggled tight against her crotch, the other cupping a breast. Her face was tight, frowning. An occasional shudder ran through her body, accompanied by a silent gasp.

On the recliner, Paul lie slumped, rigid, eyes moving at a furious pace under closed lids. His fists curled, relaxed, curled. Other than a loud exhale, the only noise he made was an angry grunt.

Earlier, both girls had received instructions. After they had planted the suggestions into Sheila and Tom, they were to find a way to disrupt the meeting at the pawnshop. They were told not to intervene personally, but to find a vessel for their master's underling to possess, and then return home. Standing next to Lisa, Cindy had a moment of clarity. She knew what she had done, that what she was going to do wasn't right. Her mind was usually muddled, her focus limited to short bursts of lucidity. It was as though she were floating in a cloud, unable to touch anything and lacking the ability to speak. When her mind did clear, she wanted her dad. Scared, alone, and not knowing where she was, Cindy couldn't understand why he didn't come for her. A fleeting image of him would appear before her. The last time it happened, he and a woman she didn't know were putting her to bed. She tried to say something, ask for help, to reach out and wrap her arms around his neck, but he was gone before she could complete the thought and she was floating again. Standing next to Lisa, Cindy shuddered, wanting her dad. *You will be together soon.* The voice in her head was gruff, impatient. She had little time to think about it—she was floating in the clouds once more.

Lisa tugged on Cindy's arm. "Let's go."

EIGHTEEN

"Yeah, keep supper warm. I'm doing one more pass, then I'll be heading home." After a short pause, Captain Bechtel added, "Give me about a half hour." When he was told the kids were already in bed, he finished the call with a warm "love you" and hung up.

While Goffstown had the reputation of being a quiet town, the past twelve months had proved it to be anything but. When it was revealed to be the home of a serial killer, the events at the Moore House put Goffstown on the national news. Feds, staties, reporters, and the curious descended, creating an inescapable circus-like atmosphere in town. While the grocery stores, restaurants, and shops benefited from the onslaught of guests, the police department found themselves dealing with crowd-control problems and lack of parking.

When the Moore House burned down after it had gained notoriety, outside law enforcement, sightseers, and the nut jobs trickled down to a manageable level; the small misdemeanors that accompanied the crowds dwindled along with them. It also freed up a squad car and patrolmen from the site, relieving the town of overtime payments to police officers. The Budget Committee might have been happy, but the officers had become accustomed to the extra money. Their grumbling went on for a few months and had only recently settled down. Bechtel had to admit he was relieved to address the normal fare for his department: speeders, drunk drivers, pub brawls, and the occasional traffic accident.

Then the kidnappings started.

Bechtel feared another circus when Manuel Chance was accused of taking those kids. He wasn't wrong. The attention Goffstown received was overwhelming, and he and his department were stretched to the limit. Releasing Chance on bond would only serve to increase the media's scrutiny. If there was any saving grace when it came to that kid going missing, it was having the State and the FBI coming in to manage the case.

He had felt guilty for thinking it, but when they found three of the children dead, he had breathed a sigh of relief none were from Goffstown. The investigation was ongoing, but his department's part in it was small.

The rape allegation against Chance was another matter.

Bechtel thought the man innocent. His dealings with him had been few, but he'd had enough contact with Chance to be doubtful he was the type to rape an old hunchbacked woman. Rape was usually a crime of violence, and Chance had never exhibited a propensity for it. Searches on his computer and home indicated he was a diligent, hardworking journalist. While his hard drive did have softcore porn on it, the images consisted mostly of topless Latino woman of middle-to-mature ages. Bechtel's gut also pointed to something else that bothered him—there was something about the Delaney woman that left him uncomfortable. Though he couldn't pinpoint it, her demeanor when he interviewed her felt off. It was also unusual that her husband hadn't accompanied her. Again, this could all mean nothing. He was not one to victim-blame or shame, and he had interviewed enough assaulted women to know they didn't all react the same way.

Bechtel flipped his turn signal and turned the steering wheel to Route 114. Passing by the cemetery, he was reminded of a notation on his desk to visit Delaney tomorrow morning to follow up with her. He assured himself he would make that appointment.

The reflection of his headlights caught movement at the far end of the cemetery.

Signs were posted at the entrance declaring the cemetery closed at 9:00 p.m., and anyone caught inside would be considered trespassers. Underage drinkers in small groups were the usual offenders, but from this brief sighting, what he saw appeared to be too small for a teenager. The urge to check it out tugged hard. He pulled over to the curb and adjusted the side spotlight to illuminate the area. Seeing nothing but gravestones, he reasoned it was most likely a dog.

A young girl stepped from behind one of the gravestones and he stiffened his shoulders. The kid stood facing the patrol car but did nothing to shield her eyes from the intense spotlight. Even from this distance, he could see who the child was. It was one of the two surviving kidnapped girls. The blond—the one who believed she was the African-American girl. He still couldn't wrap his head around their switching identities. How do two girls who have never met not only decide to become each other, but somehow manage to access each other's memories? Thankfully, it wasn't his problem. At least it hadn't been until now. The way she stood stock-still and stared made him want to put the car in Drive and get the hell out of there. Images of his wife and children ran through his head as he reached for the shift lever.

Stop. You are a police officer. You have a duty to check this out. There's no reason to be afraid.

Bechtel jumped in his seat. There was no mistaking that the voice he heard was in his head, but it was as if someone else had spoken it. A quick glance around and a study of his mirrors assured him no one else was nearby. He convinced himself that it was nerves, the voice must be his own, his conscience—the proverbial angel sitting on his shoulder telling him to do the right thing. Wherever the voice came from, it was correct, of course: it was his job to check this out. He was disappointed in himself for thinking otherwise. Switching off the ignition, he set his blue lights flashing. The spotlight remained focused on the kid. Exiting the vehicle, he gazed at the small figure standing in front of the headstone. Uneasy, his right hand settled on the butt of his gun. Blue lights splashed on and off grave markers as he walked toward the girl.

Once he was within ten feet of her, the blue lights stopped flashing off the gravestones. The spotlight went out. He craned his neck back to the cruiser. There was enough illumination from a nearby streetlight to see that the doors were closed and there was no one near the car. He aimed his flashlight toward the vehicle. Though he was too far away to make out any details, it appeared empty. A rustle near the gravestone ahead of him diverted his attention.

His reflexes kicked in. Bechtel unsnapped the strap holding the gun to its holster. A giggle from the girl pushed those reflexes into higher gear. He took a step back, crouched, and reached for his weapon.

Low to the ground, with one knee resting on grass, Bechtel's flashlight lit up the blond girl's face. She was an arm's length away.

The smile on her face inferred she was glad to see him.

Arm shaking, he lowered the gun. Keeping his eyes on the child, he replaced the firearm in the holster. The girl stared hard at him, unblinking, silent. *This is so wrong.* He was in the middle of a graveyard having a staring contest with a kid whose smile was wider than a demented clown's. He could *feel* her wrongness. His chest tightened, his nerves releasing pinpricks of pain around his heart. Desiring a physical and psychological advantage over her, he stood. The shaking of his legs gave him neither.

An odd feeling took root in his head. He could only define it as candy-brain—his thoughts were sticky, clinging to each other, invoking bittersweet emotions. Sugary syrup had encased his mind, smothering logic, preventing rational thought. Words and images jumbled, losing their meaning. Comforting images of his family appeared, crystallized, and then shattered, replaced with saccharine-laced snapshots of them in coffins. One thought did manage to break through the confectionary jumble: *the girl is causing this, get away from her.*

Bechtel stepped back from the girl. Regaining some clarity, he shook his head, ridding himself of the remaining confusion until he could think straight again.

Fuck his duty, Bechtel wanted out of there, *now.* He would radio for backup, call every damn person in the department. Wake them up if he had to. No way was he returning here and facing this girl alone. Without letting her out of his sight, he took another two steps back.

He bumped into something waist high.

It's a gravestone, he thought, *I must have walked into a gravestone.* Keeping his eyes and flashlight centered on the girl, he swung his right arm behind him to feel the object.

Instead of hard marble, his hand brushed against something light, stringy. He heard another giggle. This one behind him.

Bechtel screamed. He spun to his left and took off running. He didn't make it more than ten feet when something smashed into his back. Thrown off balance but still on his feet, he flew forward. A small pair of arms encircled his neck; an equally small pair of legs straddled his chest. Fists that should have been too small to do any damage pummeled his face. Blood seeped into his eyes and he lost his footing, and tumbled forward. As his face approached the ground, hot breath tickled his ear. A chortle followed.

Somehow, he had managed to avoid hitting the main portion of a tombstone on his way down, but not its base. The impact was intense, sending shock waves through his body, but the pain was brief.

His world went black.

No, no, no! Wake up! We have plans for you. Wake up! We have plans for you.

Lying on his stomach, Bechtel heard voices. They sounded like school children chanting a nursery rhyme. The voices were in his head. They were loud, pounding. Moments later, they receded as pain replaced them. His hands rose to his throbbing forehead; on contact, they slid off. Blood dripped from both of them. He turned over with a groan. A pair of children stared down on him. Closing his eyes, he struggled to focus his thoughts. It was coming back to him now. He had stopped at the cemetery to chase some teenagers out, only...they weren't teenagers. He remembered a young girl, a blond-haired little girl. She scared him shitless.

His eyes snapped open.

Bechtel sat up. His head spun so he crawled backward and leaned against a gravestone. He looked up. Two young girls stood there, motionless, their faces blank, staring at him. Confused, he stared back, until he remembered who they were. Desperate to be away from them, he pleaded, "I need to get back to my cruiser. I'm bleeding, I need help."

The African-American girl raised her arm. Bechtel's gun was in her hand. When it came to rest, the barrel pointed to his pelvis.

It should be too heavy for her to lift it that easy, never mind pointing it at me with a steady hand. What the fuck are these kids?

"Yes," the blond girl answered. "You are bleeding. You're going to bleed a lot more."

The officer's heart hammered. A sob erupted from his chest. "Please, let me go. What do you want from me?"

The African-American girl replied. "We want your soul, but we need your body, too." She pulled the trigger.

The bullet slammed into Bechtel's groin. His head flew back against the gravestone, his cry echoing off the other markers in the cemetery.

Once more, she fired. The bullet penetrated his stomach. His arms flew up on impact; when they fell, his head dropped along with them.

I'm going to die. I'll never see Gina and the kids again. My God, what will become of them?

Close to losing consciousness, he could still hear his murderers. One of them said, "Finish him. You need to shoot him one more time. Get the heart, stay away from his head. Do it now, someone might have heard the shots."

Bechtel's heart exploded.

The officer felt no pain. Aware of his surroundings, light surrounded him. He was floating. As he rose higher, he peered down. Battered and bleeding on the ground was his body. Two young girls stood aside it, looking up. Bechtel turned his gaze away, embracing the floating sensation. A beatific glow beckoned high above him. He was drawn to it. A believer in God and a good Catholic, he willingly gave himself up to the promise of a divine afterlife.

It was the last moment of peace he would ever experience. From below, darkness rose like smoke from an oil fire.

It swallowed him whole.

NINETEEN

The pawnshop owner placed additional metal chairs before the counter in preparation for the meeting. Rex, with Manuel in tow, returned to the shop a few minutes before nine o'clock with his own seat. It was oversized, well-padded, and capable of holding three regular-sized people. At nine o'clock, all the chairs were occupied. With the proprietor moderating, the participants listened with rapt attention to each other's stories.

"Please, hold all your comments until we've all had a chance to speak. Say something only if you want a point clarified."

Though Rex was not prone to speaking or displaying emotion, he was the first to participate, recounting his encounter at Manuel's home. When finished, he stayed silent while the others spoke.

It was close to eleven o'clock when Father MacLeod finished recounting his conversation with the demon back in Haverhill, and the instructions it had passed along. The pawnshop owner noted that the priest had pretty much stuck to the facts in the story as it had been related to him that afternoon. He left out only the personal gain he was hoping to accrue if James Moore's direction were carried out. When the priest concluded his tale with a hand flourish and a whimsical "The end", all eyes turned to the pawnshop owner.

He debated how much to tell them. His past was complicated and confusing, and he was reluctant to expose too much. He decided to share only information relevant to the reason they were all here; if they wanted to dig deeper, he would brush them off. He made eye contact with each one of them, silently preparing them for his portion of the discussion. He folded his hands on his lap and spoke.

"This shop has been in my family for many hundreds of years. We purvey merchandise of historic nature, most often purported to possess supernatural elements. Our clientele has been varied, usually collectors. While we attempt to ensure our goods do not fall into the wrong hands," his gaze settled on the priest, "we are not always successful. That's all you need to know about the shop, but it does lead us to the Prexy Box."

Everybody leaned forward, except for Rex, whose head turned to a rack behind the counter where the Prexy Box resided.

If anyone followed his gaze, they would see a framed piece of modern art on the highest shelf. It was placed there to conceal the box. The box itself had picked that location to reside. Despite various attempts to move it, it always returned to the same place. Camouflage proved useless, as it would disappear when the pawnshop owner turned his back. The painting, a poorly executed, garish combination of pastels and neon, was the only concession to stealth the box would allow. For as long as he owned the shop, only he and Rex were intimately familiar with the Prexy Box, as the pawnshop owner had often used the giant when harnessing its power.

"The box came into my family's possession in the late 1700s. Before you ask, I have never been told who originally entrusted us with the item. I can tell you that once my family became aware of its abilities, a decision was made to become its caretaker. It was—it *is*—never to be sold."

It was Paul who asked the first question. "From what we've learned tonight, it appears this Prexy Box has the power to absorb someone's soul. Whose souls does it take, and how many are in there?"

"To answer your first question," the pawnshop owner said, "monsters, inhuman and otherwise. It is the repository of pure evil. If there is a Hell on Earth, its denizens reside in the Prexy Box. As for how many, I could not guess."

Paul pushed him. "Are we talking ten, twenty, a hundred?"

"In the past two hundred years, there have been several hundred. Before that time, I cannot speak."

Manuel's mouth hung open. He blinked, and asked, "Are you responsible for tracking down these evil people and monsters and taking their souls?"

"In a word, no. I do not go looking for those or that which would harm society, or us. We are not the caretakers for the world. However, that does not stop evil from seeking out the box."

Manuel shook his head. "I don't get it. If this box captures the souls of bad guys or bad things, why would they want it?"

"The box draws evil. Many of those who've attempted to possess it did not understand its nature. They *felt*, or were told, it would channel power to whomever owned it. What most of them didn't understand is that the Prexy Box does not discriminate, it will eat any soul fed to it."

"Even the innocent?"

The pawnshop owner nodded.

Manuel added, "Do you know what happens to the souls in that box? Do the innocent and the evil wind up in the same place?

148

"I only know that those who are trapped in the box experience agony beyond belief."

Father MacLeod jumped in. "Besides you, who can feed it souls?"

The pawnshop owner inhaled sharply before answering. His gaze locked on the priest. "Whoever possesses it."

Lynne shivered. "What's to stop someone from breaking in here and stealing it?"

"All I can say is that the shop itself has safeguards and abilities to prevent intrusions. In addition, some of the items we store here are also useful in preventing theft."

The pawnshop owner froze when a series of beeps erupted from behind the counter.

"Excuse me a minute." He made eye contact with Rex, and then tilted his head toward the counter. Both men rose from their chairs, walked around the far end, and came to a stop where the beeping emanated. The pawnshop owner pushed a button and a computer rose from the counter. Standing behind him, Rex stared hard at the screen.

"That beeping you heard is an alarm from our surveillance system," the proprietor informed the group.

"He's across the street, staring at the front doors," growled Rex.

After studying the screen for a few seconds, the pawnshop owner replied. "He seems to be alone." He moved a toggle switch. "I don't see a police car out there." At the mention of a police car, the rest of the gathering stood and approached the counter. The two men at the computer kept their eyes on the screen.

"He's wobbly," said Rex. "His hand is resting on his holster."

"Why would an officer be standing there watching the front door?" mused the pawnshop owner. "It could be he saw the lights on and is simply doing a safety check. It's too dark to see his face at that distance, let's give it time before we become concerned."

"I know all the police officers in this town," offered Manuel. "Do you mind if I come back there and take a look?"

"No. Stay there." The proprietor swiveled the screen to face Manuel.

"I can't be sure, but I think that's Captain Bechtel. If it is, I for one sure wouldn't mind having him in here listening to us. According to my lawyer, he had doubts about my involvement in the kidnappings. If he hears what we have to say, not only could it help me, but he might be able to assist us in fighting whatever it is that's out to get the Prexy Box."

Father MacLeod smirked. "You want an officer of the law to believe demons are responsible for..."

Rex interrupted the priest. "He's coming."

Everyone held their breath. Seconds later they all jumped when a bang on the front doors broke the silence.

Studying the screen, Manuel said, "That's Captain Bechtel. But...there's something wrong. He's wobbly, unsteady on his feet, and his head's weaving back and forth."

The front doors of the pawnshop rattled.

Lynne whispered, "He's trying to get in."

Father MacLeod advanced to the front of the shop. "I'll talk to him through the doors, get a better look at him while I'm at it. This could be nothing, just a cop out patrolling, doing what he does."

"Stop!" The pawnshop owner's voice was loud and demanding.

The priest stopped halfway to the doors.

"Rex, I want you to escort everyone to the far side of the counter and then place them behind it. Everyone, follow Rex."

The giant didn't hesitate, though his bulk prevented him from moving quickly down the aisle between the counter and the wall. By the time he was at the end of the counter, too much time had elapsed.

The front doors of the pawnshop blew open.

Lynne screamed.

Everyone jumped back.

In a matter of seconds, both doors extended as far as they could, and then bounced back to their closed position. In the moments it was open, the pawnshop owner saw a dark silhouette standing outside the doorframe. The doors were pushed open again, and there was no mistaking who was walking in.

Captain Bechtel entered the pawnshop.

The proprietor gazed to the far end of the counter. The giant had rounded it and was on the shop floor, making his way toward the group. Loud enough for Rex to hear, the pawnshop owner said, "I'm sorry. He's all yours. I'll do what I can."

The giant nodded.

The pawnshop owner pressed a button on the counter. The walls and the floor shook. The sounds of gears whirring filled the air and heavy translucent barriers dropped from the ceiling.

As unexpectedly as it had begun, the floor stabilized. The shop went quiet.

The proprietor plunged another finger into the counter, a brief squawk overhead followed. In a tinny voice broadcast from speakers mounted in the racks, he said, "Rex, I'd be obliged if none of our guests were killed."

The giant looked toward Father MacLeod. "No guarantees," he barked in reply. Then he smiled.

Paul, with Lynne close behind him, hurried to the far end of the counter. When he reached out to grab hold and make the turn, his hand smacked into something solid. It didn't slow his momentum, however, and he crashed into an invisible barrier. Stopped dead in his tracks, Lynne bumped into him. Confused, he swept his hand over the unseen wall he was pressed against. He brushed his fingertips against the surface, smooth in some places, coarse in others. Oblivious to Lynne and the intruder, he cocked his head and focused. If he squinted, he could see etchings—words, lines, symbols, runes—floating in the air. Brushing by Lynne, he backed away and took in the entire floor of the shop. There were more of them. He reasoned the translucent barrier must run along three walls, and in front of the counter. The etchings had to be a spell of some sort, an assist in keeping something or someone from passing through it. The barrier was designed to hold something in—it was an invisible cage—and they were trapped within it.

Lynne ran her hand up against the barrier. "If this goes around the whole shop, we're stuck in here with him."

A groan came from Captain Bechtel. His eyes were opening and closing at a rapid pace; with each blink the color shifted from a dense black to a normal brown hue, and then back again. His mouth mimicked the motion, forming a grotesque smile when his eyes were wide open and black, and then a tight grimace when they closed. Soft grunts and moans accompanied the changes. As Paul stared transfixed at the man, he saw the period of dark eyes and cruel smiles lasting longer. If the officer was trying to control the process, he was losing the battle.

Abruptly, the changes ceased. Bechtel's face rested in a caricature of a smile. "Hello, everyone!" he announced. "No need to panic, I was just passing by, saw a light on, thought I'd check it out to make sure everything's okay."

"We're fine," Rex croaked.

Rex had positioned himself in front of the officer. There couldn't have been more than five feet separating them.

Bechtel's smile faulted. "You know, I don't think you are fine. See that man over there?" He pointed to Manuel. "He's a kidnapper. Stole some kids. He's a dangerous fellow."

When Manuel's mouth opened, Paul was quick to intercede. He feared an outburst from Manuel would provoke the policeman. "Officer, this man is innocent. From what he's told us, you seemed to think so, also."

Bechtel swung his head toward Paul. "Mr. Lane, you of all people should be concerned. He took your daughter. We have evidence he did some nasty things to her. Things you would have nightmares about if you knew."

Manuel turned to Paul. "NO! That's not true, Paul. I would never do that. Please, don't believe him!"

Paul nodded his head. Assuring the man, he softly said, "I don't believe him, Manny."

"Well," said Bechtel, chuckling, "it doesn't matter what you believe, I'm going to take him in for more questioning."

Rex stepped toward the officer. "I don't think so."

Though the policeman was unsteady on his feet, his arms were the definition of stability. With a deft hand, Bechtel pulled the gun out of his holster. He aimed it at Manuel, keeping his eyes on Rex.

"You need to step back, big guy. Wouldn't want me to shoot your friend here, would you?"

Rex halted and took one step backward.

"You know, we don't have to go through all this," Bechtel said. "All you have to do is give me the Prexy Box and I'll be on my way."

The speakers clicked with static. The pawnshop owner's voice followed. "We will not be doing that."

"Well then, I'm going to have to kill you one by one until you change your mind." The officer turned to Manuel. "Let's start with you."

"Wait!" Father MacLeod implored the officer. Everyone in the room turned their attention to the priest.

He continued. "First, may I ask who I'm speaking with?"

The policeman chuckled. "No."

Father MacLeod approached the officer. "Fair enough. It appears we are both after the same item. The thing is, I'm not keen enough to die for it. I have on my person an item that will allow you to take possession of it. Once you have this item, no one will stop you, no one can stop you from removing the Prexy Box and exiting this pawnshop. If you allow us all to leave, I will hand the item over to you."

The pawnshop owner's brows were furrowed, but other than that, he did not seem to be worried. His expression was one of curiosity, not fear.

The gun fired.

On impact, Manuel flew backward. Crumpling to the floor, he reached for his stomach. When he fell to the concrete, blood drained through his fingers. "God, please, help me," he moaned, but no one moved toward him. Paul stood still as a pool of red surrounded Manuel.

154

Lynne was the first to react. She ran to Manuel, bent over, and placed her hands over his and applied pressure. "Somebody, help him!"

Bechtel adjusted his aim. "Give me this item, priest. Now, or she's next."

Rex charged Bechtel.

He was fast, but not fast enough.

The gun went off. "No!" Paul shouted. Without hesitating, he rushed to Lynne. At her side, he bent over and pulled her to her feet.

"Paul, I'm okay," she said. "He didn't shoot me."

Rex had knocked over Bechtel as the gun was fired. He was lying on top of the officer's body. The cop's legs danced wildly in the air as Rex pummeled the officer's head with his fists. Blood seeped from the giant's side—and Paul knew the target of the second bullet.

Moments later, the pair on the floor stopped moving. Paul held his breath.

A silent explosion blew Rex off Bechtel. He flew through the air, his arms and legs out straight. His body hit the ceiling. He clung there for a moment and then plummeted face down to the cement floor. He didn't get back up.

Bechtel rose. Black bruises covered his face. Chunks were missing from his cheeks. Blood flowed from the wounds. His mouth hung open, exposing chipped and missing teeth. A stringy yellow fluid frothed from his lips. The officer's stance was *wrong*. He was leaning heavily to his left side, his right shoulder pushed back. It looked as if his spine had snapped. Paul wondered how in the hell Bechtel was still standing. He also noticed another thing: the gun was no longer in the man's hand. He searched the shop floor but saw no sign of it.

Bechtel rolled his head. It moved loosely on his neck until he managed to anchor it. He peered down at Rex. "Who the fuck *is* that guy?"

Rex stirred.

"Oh, no, you stay down there, big man." Bechtel levitated into the air. When he had reached five feet off the floor, he pounced onto the giant's back.

Rex didn't react. Seconds passed before he made his move; the motion was almost too quick for Paul to see. Rex's elbows shot up until his palms were flat on the floor. With a grunt so loud the pawnshop owner had to have heard it through the barrier, the giant pushed himself up. Bechtel flew off of his back toward Father MacLeod.

As crazy as everything happening was, Paul now questioned his eyesight. The officer appeared to have crashed into a new invisible barrier, landing at the priest's feet.

Bechtel glanced at the priest, recoiled, and crab-walked away from him. When the officer was a good three or four feet away, his hands went to his head. Sitting on the floor, his body rocked, only ceasing for an occasional shiver.

The barrier, the speed in which the officer scuttled from the giant, and the way Bechtel was holding himself had Paul wondering if Bechtel was physically affected by the priest's presence. Was whatever that was controlling the officer vulnerable to religious interference? His thoughts were interrupted when Rex spoke.

Standing upright, both of the giant's arms were extended, fists clenched. Blood seeped from the wound on his side, but he seemed oblivious to it. His head was turned toward the pawnshop owner. "Can we use it?" He growled.

The pawnshop owner nodded.

Paul questioned what *it* was.

156

With the fury of a bull released from its pen, Rex charged Bechtel. The giant's fists pounded the officer over and over, concentrating on his head and extremities. If Bechtel had any fight left in him, it wasn't apparent. The officer served as Rex's punching bag as his body was pounded to pulp.

Minutes later, the speaker squawked. "Rex, that's enough." The giant's assault ended. Before he walked away from what was left of the officer's body, he spit on it.

Paul couldn't believe the mess on the floor had once been a person. Blue-uniformed arms and legs—squished flat and in pieces—were detached. The officer's head was flattened, the bones in his skull reduced to small, sharp fragments. Brain matter streaked the concrete floor. The only undamaged area was Bechtel's upper torso. For some reason, the giant had avoided the area.

Startling everyone, the sounds of gears turning and the whooshing of air filled the pawnshop. Moments later, the pawnshop owner left his perch behind the counter and stood next to Rex.

"I have to ask." Father MacLeod said as he joined the two, "why didn't you pulverize all of him?"

The pawnshop owner replied without looking at the priest. "We need his heart intact."

"Why?"

"To feed the Prexy Box."

Father MacLeod's eyes lit up. "Can we watch?"

Staring hard at the priest, the proprietor answered with a terse "No."

Paul could see the disappointment in the priest's eyes. He had to admit, he was curious himself. Manuel moaned, and everyone but the pawnshop owner rushed toward him.

Lynne pulled his shirt up. "He's bleeding badly. We have to get him to a hospital, now."

The pawnshop owner spoke. "Rex, you okay for a bit?"

When the giant nodded, the proprietor walked over to Manuel. "Leave him be, I'll take care of him."

"Are you crazy?" Lynne retorted. "He needs a hospital!"

The pawnshop owner's voice softened. "Please, I'll take care of him. I need you all to leave now. I have two people to administer to, and I need privacy to..."

"Look, we need to talk some more," Father MacLeod interrupted.

"Yeah, there's more to discuss," added Paul. "Like how the hell are we going to get out of this mess? And, what about that?" He pointed to the officer's remains. "How are we going to handle that?"

The pawnshop owner stiffened. "I will take care of that," he said, "and yes, we should meet again. Come back tomorrow, two o'clock. Now, please, leave."

After Paul, Lynne, and Father MacLeod had left the building, the pawnshop owner and Rex gently lifted Manuel onto the counter. Setting him down, the proprietor went to the other side and pressed a button, and Manuel heard the faint sound of doors locking.

"Manuel?" It was the pawnshop owner. He looked into the man's eyes and smiled.

"Manny, I'm going to put you to sleep. I need you to trust me on this; I'll take care of you. You will be fine when you wake up."

Manuel sighed, then everything went black.

TWENTY

Paul and Lynne said little on the ride back to his house. Both were deep in thought, attempting to make sense of what had happened back at the pawnshop. He was sure they would discuss it once they were inside, but in the meantime, he had more questions than answers.

"Let's make sure our kids are all right, and that Sheila and Tom are out of the house before we digest all this," said Tom, at the front door. He then added, "At least I *think* they're our kids."

"They are our kids, Paul!" Lynne shot back. "Something's happened to them, something bad, and we have to help them."

"You heard what the pawnshop owner told me. He said Cindy's not my daughter. When the others told us about what happened with her at the counter this afternoon, well, it scared the everloving shit out of me. What if they're not Cindy and Lisa? What if they're gone? What if something else is inside them?"

Lynne stiffened. "Don't say that! My little girl is in there, somewhere, waiting for us to figure out how to get her back. Paul, don't give up on them, we've got to find a way." Tears streaked her cheek.

"Yeah, let's talk about this in the house."

Paul was struck how dark and quiet it was inside. Though it was late, he expected his friends to be reading or watching

159

television. He flicked on the light switch. Relief washed over him when he spotted Tom asleep on the recliner, Sheila snuggled up with a blanket on the couch.

"Lynne, why don't you check on the kids and I'll wake these guys up."

With a nod, she headed upstairs.

"Hey, buddy, we're home. Wake up."

Tom mumbled something and opened his eyes. He shook his head, attempting to clear it. When it appeared he was successful, Tom made eye contact with Paul.

Paul took a step back.

Tom's lips had straightened. His eyes had narrowed into an accusing stare.

"Whoa, buddy, you okay?"

At the sound of Paul's voice, Tom's expression softened. "I—I'm sorry, I must have fallen asleep."

"You must have been having one heck of a dream, you looked like you were ready to kill me."

Confusion now clouded Tom's face. He sighed and looked down. Paul wondered if he was trying to remember the dream.

"Sit for a minute, get your bearings. I'll wake Sheila."

He softly called Sheila's name, but there was no response. He tapped her shoulder, hoping to nudge her awake. It worked. Sheila's eyes opened. Her reaction to waking was the opposite of Tom's. She trained her eyes on Paul, a small smile framing her face.

"Hello, handsome. You're back." Sheila's smile widened.

Unsure what to make of her flirting, Paul hesitated before answering. He turned his head toward Tom, who continued to stare in thought at his lap.

Paul's attention turned back to Sheila. The wide smile was still there, but her eyesight was now directed toward his crotch.

"Um, Sheila, sorry we were late, we ran into some unexpected trouble, but we're back now. Thanks so much for watching the kids. And, ah, I know this is asking a lot of you, but can you watch them tomorrow, too? Around one-thirty, and we'll be home by dinner time."

"No problem, Paul. I'm sure Tom has better things to do, so I'll be alone tomorrow when you return. Can you lift this blanket off of me please?"

Caught off guard by the request, Paul stammered, "Yeah, sure, no problem." Grabbing the end of the blanket and pulling it off, he froze at the sight. Sheila's dress was pulled up and she was naked from the waist down, her left hand caressed her upper thighs. Paul threw the blanket back over her.

Holy shit! What the fuck was that? Did Tom see it? What the hell is going on here?

Lynne called from the stairs, "Paul, can you come here for a minute?"

"Yeah, coming."

Tom, still peering at this lap, couldn't have seen his wife playing with herself on the couch. He walked to Tom, keeping Sheila out of her husband's line of sight. "Tom, can you let yourselves out? Again, thanks for watching the kids."

Tom's eyes were hard again, his lips tight. "Sure, whatever." Tom finally gazed over to Sheila. She was standing by the couch. "Let's go."

"I'll see you tomorrow, Paul," purred Sheila.

"Sheila!" Tom barked, "I said *let's go!*"

She sidestepped past Paul and followed her husband out the door.

161

Lynne came downstairs and sat on the easy chair. "No way I'm sitting on that couch until you clean it."

"You saw that?"

"Yeah. The kids were sleeping so I left them to come back down. I was at the top of the stairs when I saw you take the blanket off her. She was doing herself, and holy shit, she wanted you to see it!"

"What the hell was that all about?"

"I saw your reaction and knew you were shocked. That's when I asked you to come upstairs. I just about died. Has she ever done anything like that before?"

Paul shook his head. "No. Never. We've joked around like friends sometimes do, nothing serious. Tom's my best friend, I'd never do anything like that!"

"I think this is part of what's happening," said Lynne. "I don't know how, but it seems too bizarre not to be."

"You think the kids had something to do with this?"

After a deep breath, Lynne let it out slowly. "I don't know for sure, but, yeah, maybe."

Paul paced the living room. "Man, I asked her to watch the kids tomorrow while we go to that meeting. If they had something to do with this, I can't expose Sheila to them again."

"Paul, we don't know if the kids had anything to do with this. It could be she had a sex dream, was horny, and wanted to throw a thrill your way."

"With her husband ten feet away?"

"Maybe, I don't know her. Different things turn different women on. If we do decide to have her come back, don't be alone with her. Make sure I'm with you at all times. We can talk to her; see if she's all right. We can decide then if we want her staying with the kids."

"Okay, we'll do that. You're still sleeping over, right?"

"Yes." After a chuckle she added, "Afraid she might come back tonight?"

"The way Tom looked, I don't think he's going to let her out of his sight. He might not have seen what she did on the couch, but I had the impression he suspects her of doing something nasty. He looked angry, with her, and me."

"Is your offer of the bed still good?"

"Yeah, I'll sleep on the couch."

"Thanks. Can we talk tomorrow morning about what happened at the pawnshop? I'm exhausted. I can use the time to think about all this while I'm falling asleep."

After saying goodnight, Tom grabbed a pillow and a blanket and brought them down to the couch. He stared at them for a moment and then dropped both onto the recliner. He went to the kitchen, got a rag, some disinfectant, and washed off the couch cushions.

TWENTY-ONE

The sun was up but not yet peeking through the windows, and Irene woke with a smile. A quick glance at the clock confirmed she had slept through the night on her back, something she hadn't been able to do since she was deformed by those four kids who she had persuaded to kidnap her months ago. Twisting her shoulders and arching her midsection, she took delight in the freedom of movement. Along with the hump, her discomfort for sleep had vanished—no more tossing and turning from side to side, no more having to breathe in Donald's foul breath, no more—

The hairs on the back of Irene's neck stood up. Cold waves brushed her shoulders, like a winter wind through an open window. The thought that she was not alone in the room overcame her and she sat up. She turned to Donald's head sitting on the nightstand. His eyes were half-closed, not focused on her, but at the wall in front of her bed. Someone else had to be in the room. She slipped her legs to the side, keeping her eyes on the only exit—the door.

No sooner had she left the bed than she discovered who was watching her.

The Dark Master stepped out of the shadows in the far corner of the room.

This was odd. He had never appeared to her unbidden, or without warning. Her uneasiness grew. Had he always had the ability to appear and hide from her? Had he done this before, and to what end?

As the Dark Master approached, its body absorbed all the available light, rendering it difficult for her to see it in the semi-darkness. Her lover had always been muscular, but now, the sinewy tissue covering its torso and arms was tighter. Its legs were trimmer, more like a jogger's than a weightlifter's. Though its penis was flaccid, it was shorter than she remembered it—the girth less capable of tearing her apart. The shade of its skin was not as dark as it had been.

The demon stopped still in the center of the room. When it leaned forward, Irene gasped. With a rustling of air, wings unfolded from its back, extending from shoulder to calf. The surface of the wings undulated as blood vessels throbbed beneath the membrane. Points, evenly distributed along their outer length, resembled the fingers of bat wings. A movement along the left wing caught Irene's attention. An appendage bobbed and floated behind it: rope-like, as thick as her fist, until it reached its end, where it morphed into the shape of a wide triangle. As it rose and fell in a rhythmic sweep, Irene realized it was the tip of a tail.

This was not the Dark Master.

This realization should have had her frightened, concerned at the least. Neither occurred. Instead, Irene's body responded to its presence. Her face flushed and her chest fluttered as her heartbeat increased. A wave of pleasure—lust—rippled through her. She shivered. Her nipples stiffened. In a submissive gesture, she fell to her knees, her eyes locked on the demon's darkened facial features. "Who—who are you?"

The demon stepped closer, the light from the window exposing its face.

It was the most handsome man she had ever seen.

Its skin was as maroon as stale blood. High cheekbones, a small nose, strong lips, and a chiseled chin, filled its features. Though hairless, not a ray of light from the window reflected off its skull or face. The demon's eyes, heavy-lidded and hazy, scrutinized her.

Having been granted the ability of illusion by the Dark Master, Irene was well aware of the powers a demon could use to possess someone. The Dark Master bestowed on her abilities that could allow her to appear irresistible to any person for short periods of time. Those four boys, Manuel, even Donald had been enwrapped to the point of ecstasy when she employed it. The thought that she might also be a victim of this type of devilry crossed her mind, but it was fleeting, gone as quickly as it had appeared. Her skin tingled with desire at the thought of subjugating herself to this demon. It stepped forward, stopping only when it towered over her. She heard a heavy intake of breath, and an equally loud exhale before it spoke.

"Bathin has claimed you. For now, your soul is his."

Though Irene had no idea who Bathin was, she assumed it was the given name of the Dark Master. A sense of loss weighed heavy on her, and tears flowed down her cheeks. "I— I can be yours. I want to be yours."

The demon laughed. "It is too late. You have made your choice. There is no changing that. No matter, in the end, you will all serve me in Hell. Give me your hand."

Irene did as asked. Her mind grew dark. Her consciousness gained weight. It floated, draining into the demon's outstretched hand. Her mind attempted to shut down at the invasion of new senses, thoughts, and visions. She was witness to Hell and its accompanying atrocities. Eternal suffering, unimaginable physical pain, and the mental anguish that

166

flourished along with them. Creatures, grotesque and stately, lorded over the carnage, reveling in the torment and torture.

The visions stopped. She hung suspended in a black void. Sounds, whispers, all rushed from the distance toward her. They invaded her, taking root, feeding her instructions. When they silenced, Irene was back in her bedroom.

She remained still for a moment, uncertain what was going on. Gazing at the floor, she realized she was on her knees, but had no idea why. Standing, she looked around. She was alone in her bedroom, naked. Confused, she walked over to Donald's head. His eyes were wide, rapidly moving back and forth.

"Excited to see me, Donald?" she teased. She placed her hands under her breasts and lifted. "I bet you miss these."

Donald's eyes continued their rapid movement.

"Well, they're the Dark Master's now." Irene chuckled and added, "As is the rest of me. I'd love to stay and talk with you, but he'll be here soon. He didn't say as much, but I think today is our big day." Something was gnawing at her, but she couldn't bring it to the forefront. She shook her head, an intuition of failure flaring in the back of her mind. *Where did this come from?* Anger overcame her. Reversing direction, she leaned over Donald's head, her face tightening. "I can't fuck this up!" she screamed. "Everything I've planned for could come down to what happens today!" Spit flew from her lips, some of it hitting Donald's lidless eyes. She shook her fist in front of him. "I am going to be his queen! Everyone will bow to me!"

After waiting for a response from her husband, Irene laughed. "Look at me, I'm talking to a fucking mute skull. I have to get my shit together." Giddy, she walked to the closet to pick out a dress. She wanted to go for a walk, clear her head, and look pretty when her lover arrived. Turning to the window, she noticed the sun was high, laminating the bedroom in bright light. Unease crept into her.

How could she have lost track of so much time?

TWENTY-TWO

The pawnshop owner sat on a stool at his counter surrounded by books on demonology and the occult. Some books were opened, some closed with blue ribbons spilling out the sides. A pile, some read, were pushed out of easy reach. Most were antiques, going back as far as the fifteenth century. They were written in Latin, Italian, Greek, and old English, which did not impede his research. Many, but not all of them, had been acquired when a consignment fell through and the owner could not be reached. A notebook filled with his handwritten scribbles occupied a space in front of him. He was pursuing the notebook when the front doors of the pawnshop opened.

"Shit deep in research, I see," noted Father MacLeod as he approached the counter with a satchel in hand. "It might please you to know, I did some of my own last night. But first, I don't see any evidence of one of our finest dismembered and scattered over your floor. And, since you seem to be preoccupied with those books, I assume your medical ministrations with Manuel and the hulk had favorable results.

The pawnshop owner glanced over to an old grandfather clock behind him. "You're six hours early. What do you want? I'm busy."

The priest laughed. "Straight to the point, huh? I guess all is well in pawnshop land. He motioned to the far wall. "Well, I think you're going to find my discoveries interesting. I logged

169

into the Vatican archives last night when I got back to Haverhill. Learned some interesting stuff. If true, it may be of some assistance to us dealing with this Prexy Box situation."

The proprietor could not tamp down his curiosity. He had been working since the early morning gathering any information he could on the Dark Master—coming up empty for the most part. There were a few leads he was pursuing, but they might be long shots; he could be wasting his time. If MacLeod had some helpful information, he could be well worth listening to.

"All right, go ahead, tell me what you know."

The priest frowned. "What, you're not going to offer me a chair?"

The pawnshop owner sighed, grabbed a stool behind the counter, and passed it over. A smile was the only thanks he received.

"Okay," the priest began, "I'm almost certain the stone you have is not John Dee's. That stone is in a London museum, vetted by the Catholic Church. Of course, they could be wrong, but that's doubtful. Their research arm is pretty damn efficient."

"Let's say they're correct," the proprietor replied. "Where did this stone come from?"

"Well, I'm not certain, but I believe I can come pretty close to guessing correctly. You see, Dee had a partner named Edward Kelley—"

"Don't bother describing their relationship, I am familiar with it."

The priest nodded. "I'll get to the good stuff, then. It seems before they had their falling out, they summoned an angel. Uriel. This angel gave them knowledge on how to build tools and devices to foresee the future. The key to building a successful shew-stone was using a language called *Enochian script*. They had moderate successes, but no home runs. It was after these first experiments, when the riches they desired weren't forthcoming, Dee and Kelley parted ways. Dee went on to make his famous scrying stone, and Kelley eventually wound up in prison. Hey, this is interesting. You want to know how Kelley died?"

"No. Unless it has something to do with that stone against the wall, I don't."

MacLeod's lips puttered and he mimicked a pout. "You're no fun. Anyway, it's obvious one of their experiments was a shew-stone. Later on, Dee called his a scrying stone to give it some separation from their earlier efforts. What you have over there," he twisted his neck to the stone, "is that first effort."

The pawnshop owner leaned back and absorbed the information.

"If your information is correct, that stone might have the ability to predict the future. To unlock that ability, someone would have to be familiar with *Enochian script*. I've never heard of it."

"I wouldn't expect you to. From what Dee and Kelley claimed, it was the language of angels. The two of them were purported to have had hundreds of hours of conversation with Uriel, and they transcribed some of them. The problem is, modern academics haven't been interested enough to study it."

"So let me guess," the pawnshop owner interrupted, "no one knows how to read it."

The priest reached into the bag he was carrying. "Enochian is a language consisting of an alphabet of symbols, many of them unrecognizable compared to other languages." He placed two sheets of paper on the counter.

The proprietor stood and stared at the papers. "Tell me some monk living in a stone hovel somewhere in the mountains, or a bored priest in the bowels of the Vatican used their spare time to decipher all of this."

Father MacLeod smiled. "Bingo! Well, kinda."

"What do you mean, *kinda*?"

"Father Golden, a nice but rather odd old guy who has a preoccupation with horror novels and slaves away in, as you put it, the bowels of the Vatican, had been assigned at one time to work on the translations. He believes his interpretation of the alphabet is close, but the problem is, he was taken off the project and never had a chance to confirm it."

"Why not?"

"Well, there was a half-assed attempt. The Vatican doesn't own a shew-stone, for one. Also, according to Dee's notes, the scrying stone in the London Museum, is *not* based on *Enochian script*. Seems he decided Uriel was holding back on him, so he looked to the *other* side for assistance. Without a shew-stone to test out Golden's work, the Church had him try out his translation on Dee's at the London Museum. Of course, they got nothing. Golden was removed from the project after that."

The pawnshop owner stared hard at the papers on the counter. "You don't know if his translation is correct, and if it is, whether it would even work."

Father MacLeod inched his head forward. "We're going to find out right now if it works."

"How? Don't tell me you learned this alphabet overnight."

The priest leaned back. "Mr. Jones!" Then added softly, "Or whoever the fuck you are, I'm hurt that you think me incapable of that."

"Cut the shit."

A chuckled escaped from MacLeod. "Okay, you're right, I didn't, but fortunately, we have Father Golden at the Vatican. Yeah, Golden is still there, occasionally toiling away on all things Uriel. I had a talk with him earlier this morning, he sounds every bit the nerd you'd imagine him to be, and he's excited that you might have the original stone. He was willing to email me a simple translated text—a short question to present to the stone to see if it works."

For the first time that week, the pawnshop owner had a glimmer of hope. If this was all true, if this worked, they could see what the future held for all of them, though he was aware that the answer could be horrific. The question then was, would they be able to alter that predicted horrific outcome? If the future could not be changed, could the information be used to mitigate any damage? He had too many questions that couldn't be answered. The best bet was to go ahead with the experiment.

"If this does work," the pawnshop owner said, "I'm not sure what we could do with the information. Knowing the future when it comes to the Prexy Box could help us put a plan of action together if the results are not to our liking. The fate of the box portends not only what happens to us in our battle with this Dark Master, but also everyone in the world. There's so much at stake here, MacLeod. I hope you've thought this through. We don't have much time. The simple question should be about the future of the Prexy Box. How did you frame this question you're going to ask the stone?"

The priest's mouth dropped. His eyes darted to the right. "Ah..."

Stunned, the proprietor said, "You're going to ask it about yourself, aren't you?" He raised his voice. "Yourself? What the hell is the matter with you? The world may be on the brink of being taken over by demons and all you can think to ask is how *you're* going to come out in all of this?"

The priest took a step back. "Whoa. Wait before you get all heated up. You seem to forget that I am playing a big part in this drama. I'm the one who's supposed to save the world by taking that box."

The pawnshop owner stiffened. "You are NOT taking possession of that box!"

"Well," said Father MacLeod, shrugging his shoulders, "I think we're going to find that out, aren't we?"

The proprietor sat back down on his stool and stared at MacLeod. What was the priest thinking? It was a selfish request. The only reason he wanted to get that box was to be done with his deal with Asmodeus. What about Celeste? The priest had to have some feelings for her.

When she had taken James Moore into herself, MacLeod could have stopped her. He had the necklace. He could have taken the demon into himself instead. The priest was the only one who knew what Celeste was about to do. Instead, he gave it to her, allowing Celeste to sacrifice herself. MacLeod was too self-centered to make that kind of sacrifice. Thinking of Celeste unearthed a deeper emotion—his fondness for the woman. He didn't know for certain, but he guessed she reciprocated. Everyone craved a partner, a mate, and it had been a long time since he had considered another one. He might never know if it was to be Celeste.

"Look," MacLeod said, "Moore said if I did as instructed, Celeste would be free of him, and she would return to us. If this question works on the stone, and we find out that I was successful with this Prexy Box grab, we might know if Celeste made it back safely. Don't you care about her?"

The pawnshop owner lowered his head. "Of course I care."

"Then let's do this."

The proprietor walked a few steps along the counter. He pressed a button and held it. "Rex, please gather Manuel and meet me in the pawnshop." There was no answer, but he didn't expect one.

Conversation between the priest and the proprietor continued until a door in the rear wall opened. Manuel stepped through, followed by Rex.

Father MacLeod's jaw dropped. "The last time I saw you, Manny, you were lying on the floor with a gunshot wound. Your blood was everywhere; I didn't think you were going to make it. Now look at you! How do you feel?"

Manuel shook his head. "I—I feel okay. It hurts a little where I got shot, but nothing like it did when it happened."

"But how?"

"I don't know. Last I remember, Mr. Jones was leaning over me. He told me the bullet was out and he was taking care of the wound. He lifted something off my stomach, it looked like a medal of some kind, and then I passed out. When I woke up, it was morning. Except for hurting a little, I'm fine."

"Can I see?" asked the priest.

Manuel lifted his shirt.

"It looks like there's an impression on your skin. It's faint, but it looks like a cross."

The pawnshop owner broke in. "It will fade."

"Whatever it was that you used on Manny could save a lot of people." The priest motioned to all the racks lined up against the wall. "In fact, I bet you've got quite a few items here that could be put to good use."

"It doesn't work that way."

With a smirk, Father MacLeod nodded. "Of course not." He turned to Rex. "You don't look any worse for wear, either. You're still ugly, though."

Rex turned to the proprietor. "Can I kill him?"

"No. Not yet anyway. We've got some work to do, and I want you two here to witness it." He explained what they were about to attempt. After answering a few questions from Manuel, Father MacLeod grabbed a piece of paper from the counter. The four of them gathered around the shew-stone. "How's this supposed to work?" Manuel asked. "It's not like you can read those symbols to the stone."

"I don't know," MacLeod answered, staring at the stone. After studying it for a few moments, Rex reached for the paper. The priest looked as though he was going to protest, but then thought better of it.

Without a word, Rex placed the sheet of paper over the large, dull circle facing them. He held it against the surface for a full minute before lifting it and handing it back to MacLeod.

The pawnshop owner was the first to notice the change in the circle. He stepped back, and the others followed.

The surface of the circle grew brighter, morphing into a clear shiny veneer. Vague shapes crept into view. The proprietor stared hard, attempting to discern what he was seeing. It wasn't long before he could make out a setting. He was quite familiar with the location coming into focus—it was the pawnshop.

The shapes continued to become clearer, defining themselves. Darker hues stood out in contrast to the lighter background. The shapes were now distinguishable. They were people.

Moments later, the shapes were in focus. Manuel and Father MacLeod gasped.

It was Manuel, MacLeod, Rex, Paul, and Lynne.

With one exception, the image was in black and white, as crystal clear as any high-definition photograph. MacLeod was standing in the center of the image, holding the Prexy Box tight against his chest. Rex, Manuel, Paul, and Lynne were lying on the shop floor around the priest. Streaks, consisting of the only color in the image—a dark shade of red— crisscrossed the floor, undisturbed by the bodies. Standing before the priest was a demon. It was huge, as black as tar. Behind the priest, at the edge of the image, stood the shadow of a man.

"The image," growled Rex, "it's moving."

He's right. The pawnshop owner observed that the movement was limited, extraordinarily slow. The only motion was the priest's.

MacLeod had been gazing down at the floor, and now he was raising his head. As if he knew he was being watched, MacLeod stared up through the surface of the stone. Though he wasn't in the image, the proprietor knew the priest's eyes were locked on his.

The image changed. The deep red blood on the floor lost its hue, the black and whites faded to gray. The people in the image lost distinction until they were blurred. The sheen on the surface dulled. In moments, the stone was as it had been before Rex placed the paper on it.

No one spoke. No one moved.

Rex was the first to react.

"Can I kill him now?"

TWENTY-THREE

The upstairs toilet flushed. Lynne was up, and though Paul hadn't heard any doors opening or closing, he knew she would have checked on the kids before heading to the bathroom. He had done the same after he had woken on the couch. Both girls had been sleeping, and he made as little noise as possible when he backed out of the room. There was a temptation to peek into his own bedroom to see Lynne, but he thought better of it. Now was not the time to introduce romantic feelers into their relationship, although despite all the crazy shit dumped on them, he found his attraction growing. He had been without a partner for a number of years now and he had believed his capacity to love died along with his wife. Doubt had weighed heavily on him that he could ever trust a woman again; besides, devoting himself to Cindy took priority over his own needs. His wife had always chided him, and...no, he had to stop thinking about his wife. Those days were in the past. What's done was done. It was time to move on.

The thing was, Lynne might not be trustworthy either. She had had an affair with a man she knew was married, and had had a child with him, no less. He had always made it a point not to judge people. Who knew why people did the things they did? But not all people were bad. Life's circumstances often forced people to make wrong, maybe even horrible choices. It would be prudent to learn more about Lynne before he allowed his feelings for her to progress. Anyway, who was he to pass judgment on her?

"Good morning, Paul." Lynne was walking down the staircase wearing his bathrobe over a long nightgown she had brought from her apartment. Her greeting was tentative, her voice raspy.

"Good morning. You sound like you didn't sleep very well."

Lynne yawned as she reached the bottom step. "I didn't. I kept thinking about what happened last night in that pawnshop. We knew that cop. He tried to help us, Paul. Seeing him possessed, dead, or whatever, and then splattered all over that shop was enough to give me nightmares." She shivered as she approached. When she was close enough to touch him, she stared deep into his eyes and asked, "Whatever was inside that cop, is it inside our kids?"

Paul's reluctance to get too close evaporated. He reached out and pulled her into a hug. She appeared to welcome the embrace by leaning her head against his chest.

"I don't know," Paul answered, his voice a little above a whisper. "I'm hoping we get some answers this afternoon when we go to the pawnshop."

Lynne nodded, her head rubbing up and down against his chest.

Breaking the intimacy she asked, "How about some breakfast?"

"Sounds good."

Breakfast was toast, eggs, and bacon, served alongside a generous portion of conversation. They discussed the events of the previous evening, compiling a list of questions for the afternoon meeting. They would occasionally bring up the condition of their girls, but would agree to hold off those discussions until they had more answers.

An hour later, the sound of footsteps scampering down the staircase brought their conversation to a halt. The girls burst into the kitchen, giggling as they asked for something to eat. *So normal,* Paul thought, *until you consider that they think they are each other and can levitate.* When the African-American girl called him Daddy and asked him for Lucky Charms cereal, it was surreal. The question slammed the seriousness of the situation back into him. He was careful to hide his anxiety.

Lynne was about to respond to the girl, but caught herself. She appeared to be as confused and cautious as he was. After breakfast, the kids went back upstairs to play. Paul and Lynne spent the morning killing time until the meeting. Both showered, spent time with the kids, and decided what to have for lunch. Just before noon, Paul turned on the television to catch the news. The report of the missing Goffstown police chief was the top story. The anchor was an overweight man with an air of self-importance who often exaggerated or diminished the importance of the stories he related. With a smugness that he tried to pass off as sincerity, he led the news with a clip of a parked cruiser with its blue lights flashing. He then related how the chief's patrol car had been discovered on the street alongside the Route 114 cemetery in the early morning. There had been no sign of the chief, but evidence of a scuffle was found inside the cemetery grounds. Interviews with other police officers and local selectmen followed, each pleading to the public to come forward with any information.

The report went on to cite the chief's investigation into the kidnapped and murdered children in the community, with the disclaimer that authorities did not know if those cases were related to the chief's disappearance.

Lynne was shaking. "They'll be coming to talk to us. What do we say?"

"If it's reporters, we brush them off. Just say we don't know anything about the missing chief, and to please respect out privacy. If it's the cops, I'm not sure what to say. We need to talk to the others, get our story straight."

"Paul, they could be here any minute. We can't wait until this afternoon."

"Yeah." Paul took a minute to think things through. "I'm going over to Tom and Sheila's to see if they can watch the kids now, or if we can bring them over there."

"Okay. Yeah, that's sounds good."

After a quick check on the kids, Paul shot out of the house, crossed the street, and knocked on Tom's door. There was no answer. He tried again, this time ringing the doorbell also. He waited. No one came.

Both cars were in the driveway, so he was sure his friends were home. It was noon; they should have been up and out of bed by now. Standing in front of the door, he debated leaving and then calling them from his house, but out of the corner of his eye, he saw a police car coming his way at the far end of the street.

He froze.

Standing on the steps of a house looking like a scared rabbit as a cruiser approached him might not be the wisest move. Even if the cop *was* driving by and not planning to stop at his house to interview him, he would certainly catch the cop's attention. *I might as well have a neon sign flashing "guilty" over my head.* Hoping Tom had left his car door unlocked, Paul walked toward it as though he didn't have a care in the world. Climbing in, he stared at the side mirror as he shut the door. The cruiser glided by without stopping. Paul took a deep breath. *My life is so fucked up.*

Less than a minute later, he was back at Tom's front door. He knocked again, this time shouting for Tom and Sheila. When no one came, he tried the doorknob. It twisted, and he pushed the door open an inch. The urge to curse himself for not having tried it earlier came and went. In its place, a prickly feeling caressed his shoulders. Something wasn't right, and he knew immediately what it was. The odor of shit and urine wafted through the crack in the door.

Paul's first thought was the dog. Though Tom was fond of the animal, Paul doubted he'd let it go to the bathroom in the house. Sheila was a meticulous homemaker—Paul's wife used to call her Martha Stewart. No way would she put up with the dog crapping in the house. Entering, he closed the door behind him and headed for the living room.

Paul stopped dead in his tracks and squinted. He wasn't sure what he was looking at. It made no sense; he couldn't process it. He stared at the scene for a few moments, taking it all in. After confirming it all wasn't a waking nightmare, denial was his first reaction.

Upended furniture, broken glass, and holes in the wall crowded Paul's vision. The odor from the feces and urine on the hardwood floor and rugs were potent, but no more than a distraction from the stage in front of him. His focus was trained on the center of the room. In an attempt to wash away the sight, he blinked several times.

A wooden beam traveled across the living room ceiling. It was a load-bearing beam, carrying the weight of the upper floors. A large eyebolt had been screwed into the beam at its center point. A rope had been threaded through its eye. One end of the rope was tied to the railing of the staircase. The other end had been fastened in a noose, wrapped around Tom's neck.

Paul's best friend hung blood-soaked, naked, several feet off the floor. A pile of shit soaked in crimson lay below his dangling feet. Clothes, the same ones he had worn to Paul's, were strewn close to the body. For some reason, Paul had the presence of mind to notice the clothes were not torn but had been cut off. Gazing at the body, he figured out why the observation came to him—*association*. Tom's penis had been sliced off, the amputation clean enough to have been done with a scalpel.

Unable to look away, Paul stood there, mentally recording everything he saw. It was a trait born from habit, having walked into too many engineering mishaps in his job. Questions formed, and for the moment, his shock was tamped down.

His first thought was that Sheila didn't possess the strength to subdue and pull on the rope to hang her husband. Someone else must have done this. Where was she? Without moving, he scanned the living room and as much as he could see of the other rooms. There was no sign of her. His next thought made him wince—*could the kids have something to do with this?* Tom and Sheila had been alone with the girls. After battling a dead cop at the pawnshop last night, anything was possible. What if—

A rattle, followed by the swish of a door opening roused Paul from his thoughts. He waited for footsteps, but the house remained silent. Someone might be upstairs. It could be whoever killed Tom, or it could be Sheila. Where was the damn dog? Paul wouldn't be averse to its presence right now. He walked to the bottom of the stairs and called out Sheila's name. There was enough distance between himself and whomever was upstairs to make a run for it if he needed to.

He received an answer.

"Yes." It was Sheila's voice.

The reply wasn't in the form of a question; it appeared to be an acknowledgment. The tone was even, the volume low, but loud enough to hear. There was no trace of fear.

He wanted to scream at her. Ask her if she knew that her husband was downstairs, dead, hanging from a rope. How could she not know? Should he ask her if she was okay? Was she tied to the bed? Hurt, bleeding? But it was the way she responded that had him discarding all of those options. She sounded matter-of-fact, preoccupied.

"I'm coming up," he said.

Once again, she answered with a single word. "Gooood."

She exaggerated the word, extending it. He had the impression she was playing coy, seductive. An image of her popped into his head: on his couch, the blanket lifting from her body. He shook it away. *She must not know what happened to Tom, or she'd be flipping out right now.* This meant he would have to tell her. He swallowed hard and climbed the stairs. At the top, he noticed their bedroom door was ajar.

"Sheila, it's Paul. I'm outside your bedroom door. Are you okay in there?"

"Uh huh."

"I need to talk to you, can I come in?"

"Of course."

Paul pushed the door all the way open. He stood in the doorway.

Sheila was sitting up against the headboard with her eyes closed. She was wearing a sheer nightgown, and a blanket covered her from waist to toe. When Paul's eyes went to her deep cleavage and erect nipples, it was a fleeting glimpse; guilt dictated he lower his eyes.

"Sheila, it's me, Paul. We need to get out of here. Now."

There was no answer.

"Come on, Sheila, I'm not kidding."

She lay still, as if she hadn't heard him.

"You can't be sleeping, I just heard you." Paul closed his eyes for a moment. *What the fuck am I going to do?*

He heard a thump downstairs.

Oh fuck!

He had to get Sheila out, now. Paul closed the bedroom door until he heard the latch click, and locked it. Hurrying to the side of the bed, he put a hand on her shoulder and shook her lightly.

"Sheila...Sheila, come on, get up."

Paul jumped back. Sheila's head fell forward, her chin resting on her chest. This time when he stared at her breasts, it was to detect any rising and falling. They were not moving.

"Sheila?"

He knew what he had to do, though years of watching movies and reading novels had taught him it was a bad idea. Pulling the blanket off would confirm his fears. He knew her lap would be soaked with fresh blood, indicating the killer was still in the house. Still, what choice did he have? Shaking, he reached out and grabbed hold of the end of the blanket nestled under her breasts. He silently counted, and when he got to three, he pulled.

Paul wasn't sure what he was seeing. There was blood, as he feared there would be, but it wasn't as much as he'd expected: spots on the sheet between her legs and small stains on her thighs.

Sheila's hands were cupped, her red-splotched fingers holding something tight, inches from her crotch. None of those movies or books had prepared him for what it could be. The guess came to him on his own, the image causing him to moan

185

loud enough for anyone downstairs to know he was here. The thing was, it was a guess, but he had to know for sure. It would confirm that no one was downstairs and that somehow, Sheila had had the strength to murder and castrate Tom. On top of that, as crazy as it sounded, she was in their bed holding on to her husband's severed penis.

Paul was close to vomiting, but the compulsion to find out what was in Sheila's hands was too strong to ignore. He leaned over, reached toward her.

Sheila's cupped hands flew to her groin.

Paul stammered a curse and pulled his hand back.

The tips of Sheila's curled fingers pressed down forcefully, then backed off. The motion was repeated again and again, the pace quickening. Her eyes were still closed, her chin still resting against her chest. *Is she masturbating? She wasn't breathing! Dead people don't masturbate!*

Paul screamed, backing away until he hit the wall. Sheila's chin lifted off her chest. She was staring at him. Her eyes were wide open, impossibly so, convulsing in their sockets. Her mouth, stretched open to its fullest, was set in a rictus of perversion. Both rows of teeth, exposed to the molars, possessed red meaty bits nestled in the gaps. Her tongue, thrust out and stiff, retreated to the corners of her mouth and then stuck back out. Paul heard the sounds of cartilage crushing as she twisted her neck ninety degrees to follow him with her bulging eyes.

"Paul, don't run away. Don't you want to see what I have in my hands?" Her voice was soft, sweet, enticing. "Come on, I know you do." The wall prevented Paul from pushing away farther from her, but it didn't stop him trying. His arms scrambled against it, his ass pressing hard on its surface in the unlikely event the wall would give. Repulsed at the sight, his entire body shook, but he couldn't take his eyes off her.

"Oh, come on, Paul, don't be afraid. I won't hurt you. I've wanted to fuck you for so long. You know that, don't you."

It was not a question. Despite his fear, somewhere in the back of Paul's mind, he found himself agreeing with her. He wished to God it wasn't true.

"Let me show you what I have in my hands. This will prove my love for you." Sheila lifted her arms. Holding the object up high, she said, "Tell me I'm wrong, but I'm guessing you knew what it was all along, didn't you, dear? I hope yours is bigger."

Paul's legs weakened, and he slid to the floor. "No, no, no!"

"I don't need this anymore, Paul, now that I have you." She tossed the severed appendage toward him. "You can feed it to the dog if you want. Oh, wait, no, you can't." Sheila giggled.

The dog?

The mention of the dog opened a hole in the fog of fear engulfing him. Sheila had killed it, just like she had killed Tom. Images of his best friend playing with the dog flashed into Paul's head. Now they were both dead. No. Wait. Sheila wouldn't have—*couldn't* have—killed them. Something else inside her did.

Whatever it was, it had killed her, too.

Whatever it was might also be in his little girl.

Thoughts of Cindy grounded him. He straightened up, forced himself to look away from Sheila, and rushed toward the bedroom door. The knob wouldn't turn.

Sheila called after him, her voice now guttural, masculine. "You can't save Cindy. She's mine already. She needs comforting, Paul. Let me bring you to her."

The lock!

Paul's fingers fumbled on the knob until they found the button. He twisted it, the door opened, and he shot through. At the top of the stairway he tensed, expecting to hear that low, growling, guttural voice behind him as he ran down the stairs, but the only sound was his footsteps on the wooden treads. It wasn't until he was at the bottom that he recalled the thump he had heard earlier. Was someone else in the house? Holding on to the banister, he abruptly stopped

Paul held his breath.

The scene before him was in sharp focus, but it was receding into the distance. His mind was shutting down—it wanted no part of what he was seeing.

Down from the beam, Tom was kneeling, petting the dog. One end of the rope lay twisted on the floor, the other still wound tight around his neck. The animal's belly had been slit open, intestines making a trail from the kitchen. Its eyes were missing, bottle caps from beer bottles shoved into the empty sockets. The dog's lower jaw was broken, hanging down to the floor. Paul didn't see a tongue.

"Paul," Tom said, "you're the reason for all this." The statement was casual, with no sense of remorse. The dead man's hand caressed the body of the dog. "Damn," he said as he gazed at his pet. "I loved this big guy."

Paul's breath returned. "Wh—what do you mean this is my fault?"

What passed for a smile adorned Tom's mouth. "You've been fucking Sheila. I couldn't let that go on."

"No! No, I never did. Tom, you've got to believe me."

"Oh, don't lie. Last night, while I was at your house, it came to me. I saw everything. The things she did to you, and all the different ways you had her. She was never like that with me. I have to admit, I was jealous."

188

Paul shook his head. He pleaded, his voice strong, but then trailed off when he realized he was talking to a dead man. "None of that happened! Something got inside you, made you see, those—those things."

Tom continued to stroke the dog. "You know, you two can be together again if you want. It can happen. All you have to do is help me out. I need something, and you are in a position to get it for me."

The Prexy Box!

"No."

"If not Sheila, how about Cindy? Be nice if she was back in her own body, wouldn't it?"

Paul grimaced, his hands clenched. His stomach churned. He was tempted for a moment, but only for a moment. This demon—or whatever this thing was—had killed his best friend. One of its kind possessed a cop who had died a violent death in the pawnshop. It was all violence, lies, heartbreak— their stock in trade. Also, this demon knew about Cindy and Lisa, but Father MacLeod had told them that demons were unable to possess more than one person at a time, rendering its offer useless. More lies. These fucking things were seeking a way to enslave all living souls. To say it couldn't be trusted was an understatement. He gave his answer again.

"No."

"Well, then," Tom said, "I guess I'm going to have to kill you, too."

The dead man rose from the floor and the eviscerated dog scrambled to stand. Paul bolted from the bottom of the stairs to the front door. It opened easily. Outside, he flew down the front walk without looking behind. When he reached his own front door, he slipped inside and locked it. He peered out the glass window in the door to see if he had been followed.

He hadn't.

Sighing with relief, he turned toward the living room. Lynne was sitting on the recliner, staring at him. The girls were expressionless, seated on the couch, their eyes also trained on him.

"Are you okay?' Lynne asked.

"We've got to talk," Paul replied, then whispered, "alone." He swung his head to the girls. Cindy and Lisa were smiling.

TWENTY-FOUR

Irene took advantage of her newfound mobility by taking a long walk around the property. She wasn't sure if it was because she didn't want to be alone or because of her macabre sense of humor, but she had placed Donald's head in a little red wagon to accompany her. Maybe it was a little bit of both. She delighted in her husband's suffering. *What must he be thinking?* she wondered. *Reduced to no more than a lump of bone and brain matter and a staring pair of eyes, he'll never get to walk on his own again, work on the barn, eat the fruit from his gardens.* She assumed he might feel the warmth of the sun against what was left of him, maybe even smell the wildflowers dotting the property, but it might only add to his misery. That was fine with her.

Despite the ability to walk unimpeded and the satisfaction she took from Donald's anguish, an air of uncertainty clung to the edges of her mind. She recalled having woken up that morning, refreshed, and gazing at the clock. It had read 6:00 A.M. The next thing she could remember was talking to Donald and then getting dressed. The clock had read 12:00 P.M. Six hours were lost to her, and she hadn't a clue what she had done during that time. She might have gone back to sleep, though she would have remembered that.

The more she mulled it over, the more concerned she became.

Had the Dark Master come to her? If so, did he remove the memory? Worse, did *she* block out that time from her head because she couldn't deal with what he had said? She dismissed the thought. What could he have said that was so jarring she wanted to forget it? After all she had been through with him, nothing could have frightened her that much. The only exception would have been if he decided to abandon her. That didn't seem likely. He would have killed her, and she was obviously still here among the living. She decided not to ask him if he had visited her this morning. If he mentioned it in a conversation, she would go along with it. Make something up if he challenged her. The last thing she wanted to do was to sow doubt in his mind. Still, despite these misgivings, she wanted him—here and now. She found herself calling to him in her mind.

A breeze sprung up, the bottom of her dress fluttered, and the wisps of her hair took flight. It carried with it an odor she was familiar with—burnt matches. Before her, a rippling void appeared, the light within it fading. A dark figure coalesced inside a murky cloud at the center of the undulating air. Its metamorphosis continued, manifesting itself into the physique of a tall, muscular man.

The Dark Master had come for her.

"Irene," the demon said, its tone as hard as the expression it wore. "Are you ready?"

With the exception of when those boys took her, the demon had never appeared to her outside of her house. When it had come to her at home, she thought his close proximity as intimate. Seeing it from this distance, outdoors no less, allowed her to view it from a new perspective. She had always marveled at its physical structure and the power it radiated, but here, her awe and sexual lust for it was overpowering.

Was she ready? She had never been more ready in her life. She lifted her dress to her thighs and sunk to her knees. She pulled the hem higher.

"No," the Dark Master admonished her. "That's not what I meant."

Confused, Irene let the dress fall from her hands.

"You are to procure the Prexy Box today. The one who possesses it is making plans to deny us. We have to stop him, now."

Irene's nerves ignited. She had been waiting for this moment for so long, now it was here. "Tell me what to do, where to go."

The Dark Master stepped forward, the turbulent air following him. He placed his hand on her head.

Irene closed her eyes. Minutes later she opened them. Spirals of unending darkness swirled in the sockets.

She was ready.

TWENTY-FIVE

Paul sat on the recliner, relating to Lynne what had happened in his best friend's home. "When I walked in, Tom was hanging from a beam in his living room, one end of the rope was tied to the stairway, the other around his neck. There was no stool, no chair, nothing he could have stepped on to hang himself."

Lynne stood in front of him, shaking her head and frowning. How could this be true? She had seen Tom last night, hours ago. Confused, she pressed Paul. "I don't understand. That doesn't make sense. How did he hang himself?"

"My first thought was that Sheila did it." Looking away, he added, "But I had no idea how she had the strength."

"Sheila? Why Sheila?"

Paul shivered. "His penis was cut off."

Lynne gasped. Leaning over, she grasped Paul's hand and pulled on it, indicating she wanted him to stand. When he was up, she stared deep into his eyes. "I need you to tell me everything that happened there." She led him to the kitchen, sat him on one of the chairs at the table, and sat next to him. Still holding his hand, she said, "I need to hear it all."

Paul recounted his experience at Tom and Sheila's. Lynne kept her eyes trained on his; she saw disgust and fear in them as he described what happened. When he had finished, neither of them spoke for a few minutes.

Straining to sit up from his seat, Paul muttered, "We have to call the police."

Lynne put her hand on his shoulder and pressed. "Whoa. Wait. Let's think about this."

"What's to think about?"

"We have to go to the pawnshop, remember? Those guys are our only chance of figuring out what's going on." Lynne hesitated before continuing. "Paul, as terrible as this sounds, what happened over there could be something's way of trying to keep you from meeting with them."

Paul's eyes widened. "Holy shit. Tom and Sheila were killed because of me."

"What the fuck, Paul! *Us*, they might have been killed because of *us*! I'm as much a part of this as you are." A single tear streaked down her cheek.

Their eyes met. "Yes, of course. I'm sorry." He rose from the chair and hugged her. "What the hell are we going to do?"

Lynne broke the hug and backed away from him. "For starters, we *will* call the police, but only after we go to the pawnshop. If we call them now, we'll be questioned through the night. Second, we have to decide what to do with the kids. I've thought about that, and I've come up with the only answer that makes sense."

"What's that?"

"We take them with us."

TWENTY-SIX

Though the image had faded, Manuel couldn't take his eyes off the stone. It was unreasonable to think it could happen, but he was hoping it would switch back on, show them an alternate version of the future, one where they weren't dead, bleeding out on the floor. Rex's question about killing the priest snapped him back to the present, and he wasn't ashamed to admit the giant had a good idea.

"No," the pawnshop owner answered, "although the idea is tempting."

MacLeod's eyebrows lifted, but he said nothing.

The proprietor broke from the group and started for the counter. "For two reasons," he continued. "First, if the stone does in fact foretell the future, I don't think we can change it."

His voice gravelly, Rex broke in. "Let's find out."

"I don't think so, Rex," the pawnshop owner said as he made his way behind the counter and sat before all his research books. "If you tried to kill him, something would happen to prevent it, and, for all I know, the result would be what we just saw. I prefer to delay that for as long as possible."

"What's the second thing?" Manuel asked.

"The second thing is we may be able to use what we saw to our advantage."

MacLeod spoke up. "I think I know what you're getting at. If the future can't be changed, maybe we can manipulate it. What if we mimic what we saw? We stage the scene. Perhaps that is what we saw on the stone."

The pawnshop owner's face tightened. "That's not happening. I told you before, there's no way I'm giving you the Prexy Box."

"Oh, come on," the priest retorted. "It might be the easiest way out of this."

"Maybe not." The proprietor paused a moment. "Think about what we saw. Yes, there was blood, but whose? I didn't see any wounds on us."

The others murmured their agreement.

"And, did any of you notice the shadow in the image?"

"I saw something," admitted Manuel, "but I couldn't tell what it was. Now that you mention it, I guess it could have been a person, but it didn't look normal. The image was black and white, but this was darker than the rest of the image."

Nodding, the pawnshop owner went on. "Yes, and I can't say for sure, but it seems someone or something else might currently be in play for the Prexy Box."

The priest shuddered. "It could belong to this Dark Master."

"I think the black demon we saw in front of MacLeod *is* the Dark Master," replied the pawnshop owner. "We need the Dark Master's demon name so MacLeod can do what he does and send him back to Hell. If this image actually is the future, the priest is the only one left standing—the only one of us between the demon and the Prexy Box. As much as I'm loath to admit," he said, pointing toward MacLeod, "you might be the only person who can save mankind."

The priest had a one-word reply. "Fuck."

"We've only a couple of hours before Paul and Lynne arrive, I'd like to do some more research on who this Dark Master is. MacLeod, I would like you to assist me. Can you call your contacts at the Vatican to see if anyone there knows who the hell this demon could be?"

"Yeah, I can do that."

"Rex, I'd like you and Manny to station yourselves outside the pawnshop. Keep an eye out for anything unusual. The range of the cameras is limited."

Rex motioned for Manuel to follow. As they walked to the front doors, the pawnshop owner told MacLeod to hold off for a minute before calling the Vatican.

"MacLeod," said the proprietor, "last night when the police chief attacked us, I noticed something odd."

"Odd? You're kidding, right? Everything about last night was odd."

"When we were fighting him off, Rex threw him and he landed next to you."

"Yeah? So what?"

"His reaction was noteworthy."

MacLeod broke off eye contact. "How so?"

"He scurried away from you. It appeared he couldn't be in the same proximity as you."

"I did notice that. It might have something to do with my profession. The possessed have never taken a liking to me."

"Also, in that image we saw on the stone, how come you're the only one standing? Why you?"

MacLeod sighed. "How the hell do I know? Look, if you've got something on your mind, come out with it."

"The necklace, MacLeod. The one I gave to Celeste to protect her from the demons at the Moore House."

"What about it?"

"You collected Celeste after she took James Moore inside her and brought her to Haverhill. From what you've told us, she's the one who's holding on to the demon, so there is no need for the necklace to protect her. You've had the opportunity to take that necklace. Though you've denied it, I think you're lying."

The priest's shoulders stiffened and he looked away. The pawnshop owner knew the next words out of MacLeod's mouth would be another lie.

"Look, Mr. *Jones*, I don't like being called a liar. You want to search me?"

The pawnshop owner's gaze traveled from the priest's head down to his belly. It was all he could see of the man because of the counter. Now was not the time to challenge MacLeod. He might need the priest to banish the demon—if they could get its name—and he didn't want to run him off. However, he did want the last word.

"MacLeod, I want to remind you the necklace is mine and, if you do have it, I want it back."

The priest grinned. "Noted. Can I make that phone call now?"

Without waiting for an answer, the priest left the counter, walked to the far side of the pawnshop, and pulled a phone out of his pocket. The pawnshop owner smiled behind the priest's back. Not only was he sure MacLeod had the necklace, he was glad of it. It could prove useful later on.

TWENTY-SEVEN

Manuel stood outside the pawnshop, keeping a lookout for Paul, Lynne, or any threats. He was also searching for Rex.

A half hour ago, as they walked outside, Manuel was having a one-way conversation with the giant and, when he turned to face the big guy, he was gone. Confused, Manuel walked the length of the storefront trying to locate him, but he was nowhere to be found. Manuel thought about going back inside to alert Mr. Jones. He hesitated, though, thinking through what he knew about the giant.

When Manuel had walked from the police station the day before, he had had a feeling of being watched, but didn't see anyone. It turned out to be Rex. The man was adept at concealment. Thank God, as he had saved Manuel from the clutches of Irene, or a projection of her, anyway. He still didn't understand if she had been there or not. The thing was, Rex was good at hiding in plain sight, and that wasn't a bad thing. The attention garnered by a giant standing in front of a shop would be distracting and garner attention. If something were to attack them, innocent people could get hurt.

The thought of being attacked brought to mind the image Manuel had seen on the stone. He was one of the people on the floor, surrounded by blood. His first thought had been, *That's how I die*. The notion unsettled him, and he had difficulty coming to terms with it. When the pawnshop owner pointed out there were no visible wounds on the bodies, only then did he allow his despair to recede. While the man's words weren't exactly comforting, they did offer some hope, and lately, hope had been in short supply.

Manuel's left shoulder dropped like a stone. Lost in thought, it took him a second to react. He yelped and shuffled forward. Spinning around, he saw a massive arm outstretched toward him with its hand open, palm down. It was Rex, standing over him. The giant gestured to the right.

Exiting a car in the parking lot of the hardware store were Paul and Lynne. When they closed their doors and opened the two rear ones, Manuel shook his head in disbelief. They had brought the demon-infested kids with them.

"Wait here. Don't let them in," Rex commanded before he slipped back into the pawnshop.

Inside, MacLeod wandered back to the counter. "I spoke to one of our experts on demonology, a priest by the name of Father Rainey. I asked him if there was any reference to a Dark Master in any of the ancient documents. I expected him to tell me it would take days or weeks to check, but he told me to hold on. It turns out the Vatican has been spending the last fifteen years scanning and downloading ancient texts in their archives. Not all of them, of course, they're still working on the project, and not all of the documents have been downloaded, yet."

"And?" the pawnshop owner asked.

"And, he said he would do a quick search on what they have. Computers are so fast nowadays, do you know he told me—"

"Get to the point, MacLeod."

The priest handed over a piece of paper. "Father Rainey came up with five matches. He spelled them out for me and I wrote them down. Uh, you know not to say those names out loud, right?"

The pawnshop owner nodded as he glanced at the paper. Five names, capitalized, with dashes between the letters.

B-E-R-I-T-H
S-O-N-E-I-L-L-I-O-N
B-E-E-L-Z-E-B-U-B
A-Z-U-S
B-A-T-H-I-N

"Here's the thing," continued MacLeod, "while all five of these names came back with a hit on *The Master* or *The Dark* in their attributions, none of them contained *The Dark Master*. And, as I said, these are only hits from what's been downloaded, there is much more still sitting in the vaults. You can also add to this that some texts have not been studied, or even cracked open in the last couple of thousands of years. By no means is this list definitive."

"It's more than we've got, so we can start with these. Can you access the database at the Vatican to look these names up?"

"I can try. I'll have to talk to the right people to get the passwords to let me in. It could take a while."

"If we find ourselves under assault beforehand, can you do anything with what we know?"

MacLeod shook his head. "The demon must be in my presence for the exorcism to work. If not, reciting any of these names would have the opposite effect."

"You'd summon them?"

"Yes."

"MacLeod, I've got two questions about the list. The first is, how come Lucifer isn't on it? I'm assuming it was there and you took it off."

The priest grinned. "Yeah. From what James Moore told me back in Haverhill, we can assume it's not Lucifer."

"Okay, that makes sense. Let me ask you this, why can we speak Lucifer's name and Beelzebub's name aloud without those demons manifesting themselves?"

MacLeod's grin faulted. "That's an excellent question and you're obviously not the first person to ask it. From what I've been taught, those names are used so often in everyday speech and literature, both those demons would be popping up like a whack-a-moles all over the world. They'd never have the time to wreak their havoc. Those names have become, in a term you might understand, *generic*. If you want to summon either one of those demons, you've got to put some work into it."

The pawnshop owner took a moment to digest the priest's answer before responding. "Time isn't on our side. You get moving on calling the Vatican." He pointed to the stacks of books on the counter.

"I'll work with these. It should be easier now that I have some names to work with. I'll also try the internet."

The proprietor didn't have a chance to finish the sentence. Rex pushed open the front doors of the shop with enough force to slam them against the inside wall.

"We got a problem."

The pawnshop owner sighed. "Now what?"

TWENTY-EIGHT

Paul approached the pawnshop holding the African-American girl's hand. As incredible as her claim was, Paul *was* beginning to believe her. The young girl's memories, movements, and inflections were all those of Cindy. When he heard her playing upstairs or in another room with Lisa, their conversations and laughter were familiar, comforting; however, those emotions were inevitably upstaged by doubt and unease when confronted with their physical appearance. After discovering the bodies of Tom and Sheila this morning, his feelings for the girl took a more ominous turn—he was afraid of her. Lynne was adamant there was something left of Cindy in the girl, but the grin the girl fixed him with had all but slammed the door shut on that. There might still be a chance his daughter was buried somewhere in the child, buried deep, but he found himself coming to the realization that Cindy was gone. Dead.

Holding the girl's hand only reinforced that feeling—there was no life in it. Her grip had all the familial warmth of a mannequin.

"It looks like we're not the only ones who are early," remarked Lynne as she spotted Manuel in front of the pawnshop.

Manuel waved to them, but his hand stopped with the palm facing them.

"He wants us to stop," whispered Lynne. "That's not good."

When they caught up to him, Paul took the initiative. "Hey, Manny. What's going on?"

Manuel looked nervous; his eyes darted from the children to Paul, and back. "I was told to wait out here for you," he replied. "Rex wanted to let Mr. Jones know before you brought the children in."

"Well," Paul said lightly, "that's too bad."

"What's too bad?"

Without another word, Paul pushed Manuel to the side. "Come on, Lynne, let's talk about this inside." Pushing the doors open, he led her and the children into the pawnshop. He didn't get far. Rex was standing before them. Paul stopped short when he saw the determined expression on the giant's face.

The pawnshop owner defused the situation. "Rex, let Paul in, keep the others there if you would."

Paul circled around the giant and approached the counter. "Why did you bring the children?" The pawnshop owner's voice was calm, but direct.

Paul related the events of his trip to Tom and Sheila's. When he had finished, he added, "We have no choice. I couldn't leave them alone with Lynne. We need to be here, Mr. Jones."

The priest jumped into the conversation. "We should have expected this. The stone had Paul and Lynne in the image. This means there's more than a good chance what we saw is going to happen today."

"Stone? Image?" Paul was confused. "What are you talking about?"

While MacLeod explained, the pawnshop owner gazed at a monitor on the counter and remained silent. When the priest finished, Paul whispered, "Oh my God! We are going to die today."

No one argued with him.

The proprietor, deep in thought, must have come to some conclusion about the children as he called to Rex to let Lynne and the kids in. They all headed to the counter with Manuel following. When they reached it, the pawnshop owner directed his attention to the children.

Cindy and Lisa stared hard at the proprietor, their faces neutral. For Paul this was more frightening than the grins they sometimes flashed. The proprietor's expression was similarly blank. After a few tense moments, he addressed them.

"Girls, I want to speak to your parents alone. It won't take long. Would you mind stepping over to the rack by that wall?" He pointed. "You might find something that will interest you."

Breaking eye contact with the pawnshop owner, the children faced each other. An unspoken agreement had them nodding. "Sure," said the white girl, "but I hope it doesn't take too long, I want to be with my mommy." Without waiting for a reply, the two left the group and made their way to the rack.

The pawnshop owner asked the adults to step back. Once they did, he pressed a button recessed in the counter.

Paul jumped as the sound of the clicks to the front door engaged. The whirling of gears and ceiling panels sliding filled his ears. He caught wisps of the translucent panels as they slid from the ceiling to the floor. Other barriers, these ones visible, dropped over the windows and in front of the doors. Lynne raced to the children only to crash into a translucent wall before reaching them. Rubbing her head, she reached out and slid her hand over a surface she couldn't see. Paul recalled the cop entering the pawnshop the evening before, so he understood this was a means of protection for the pawnshop.

Alarmed, he scoured the area, fearful of an attack. Seeing nothing, he lunged toward the counter to ask what was going on and he slammed up against a translucent barrier. Stunned, he took a moment to settle himself, then checked to see if the others were as panicked as he was.

They were staring at him with their eyes wide. "I—I'm okay," he mumbled. The children were motionless, their eyes narrowed, trained on the pawnshop owner. *They look pissed.* He called out to Lynne and she turned. Before he could say another word, a sound at the front of the pawnshop had them both turning toward it. After he heard it a second time, the doors imploded.

TWENTY-NINE

While MacLeod explained to Paul about the image in the stone, the proprietor's attention had been focused on a surveillance monitor. In the garden section at the far end of the hardware store's parking lot, a white-haired woman in a long sundress stared at the pawnshop. One arm by her side, she cradled something in the other—indistinct but large. He thought it odd that not one customer acknowledged her presence. It was if she were one of the cement birdbaths lined up for sale.

The pawnshop owner toggled a switch to zoom in on the woman. When a clear image came into view, he froze. Disheveled hair framed her features, highlighting her round face and oval eyes. They were as large as eggs. Completely black. He found himself leaning toward the monitor, peering at them, lost in their depth. It shouldn't be possible at this range, the camera wasn't that powerful, but he could see even darker spirals swirling in the emptiness.

In the background, Paul's voice cut through the hypnotic pull. "Oh my God. We're all going to die today."

The proprietor pulled back and averted his gaze from the camera. The spirals remained imprinted on his irises and he blinked to banish them. Before alerting the others, he wanted to check out what the woman was holding. He toggled the switch down, settling the view on her midsection. Not sure of what he was seeing, he zoomed in as much as he could without distortion. When he identified it, his blood ran cold.

It was a skull.

There was little time to act. He needed to separate the children from the rest of them, after that, he needed everyone else to stand at least a foot away from the counter. When both were accomplished, he pressed buttons recessed into the counter. He had no time to inform them about the woman before the front doors imploded.

Glass and steel slammed into the translucent barriers protecting the pawnshop.

The barriers held.

Twisted beams, shattered glass, and remnants of the entrance awning pressed tight against the clear partitions, blocking the view. He toggled the surveillance switch to aim the cameras onto the front doors.

The woman from across the street now stood on the other side of the wreckage, staring directly into the camera.

"Rex!" The proprietor's voice was steady, but even through the loudspeaker, no one could deny its urgency. "There is a woman outside the front doors. Prepare for an assault. I would advise the rest of you to move to the rear of the shop."

Lynne rushed to the children. "What abou—?" Both girls were touching the translucent panels. Their hands clawed at the barrier, attempting to break through. It wasn't the blood on their fingertips or the scratches appearing to float in the air Lynne reacted to—it was their eyes. They were wider, blacker than anyone would think possible. Both their mouths were open, the cavities as dark as their eyes. She backed away from them. "Paul?"

The pawnshop owner interrupted before Paul could react. "Stay away from them, damn it! Get to the rear of the—"

On the other side of the front door, rubble went into motion. Snatches of daylight poked through as twisted metal beams, remnants of the awning, and darkened glass ripped away from the translucent barrier. On the monitor, the woman's arms were in motion. With a wave of her hand, pieces of debris jettisoned from the doorway onto the sidewalk. Like a macabre conductor orchestrating the tempo of their deaths, she swung her arms through the air to clear a path. When the last piece of rubble sailed to the sidewalk, the pawnshop owner didn't need the monitor to observe her. She stepped toward the barrier until she was inches from it.

Manuel was the first to comment. "Duck Lady!" he gasped.

Irene touched the barrier. Her fingers slid across its surface. Though her empty black eyes looked straight ahead, the pawnshop owner had no doubt she saw everything. Moments later, those black pits swung toward him. In a matter of seconds, her gaze lifted to the highest shelf on the rack. She smiled.

"Rex," the proprietor shouted into the microphone, "we can't let her get the Prexy Box."

With clenched fists, the giant squared his shoulders and leaned his massive bulk toward the front of the pawnshop.

Irene placed her palms against the barrier. Her fingers hooked, and she pressed. Ten small circles appeared on the panel. They elongated as she pushed her fingers deeper.

What the hell, thought the pawnshop owner, *that's three inches thick.*

A sound like cracking glass echoed through the shop. The woman's fingers had broken through the barrier. Irene lowered her hands. Fissures, extending through the panel, followed in the wake of her falling digits. When the fissures reached her hips, she bent her knees and continued to plow

210

furrows through the barrier. After reaching the floor, she stood and repeated the action.

"She's weakening it," shouted Father MacLeod. "She's going to break through. Is there anything you can do?"

The pawnshop owner stared at the priest. An idea came. He squatted and searched the console under the counter. Earlier, a button recessed in the counter had set in motion the entirety of the shop's defenses. He could reverse the process with the push of another button. The console gave him the option of choosing which individual panels to lower and which to lift. He reached for the button that controlled the panel to the front door. He hesitated. If he pressed it and his plan didn't work, it would be the equivalent of inviting her in.

He poked his head over the counter. The woman's hands were high above her head, working their way down. She had successfully carved out two more rows of grooves, and she was working on the third set. Within minutes, she would break through.

If he was going to do it, he was running out of time.

He pressed a button.

The panel protecting the front doors lifted. Sounds of gears meshing and pulleys whirling rumbled through the shop. These defenses were built with speed in mind, and while everything happened quickly, the proprietor knew what to look for.

With her fingers stuck in the panel, the woman was lifted along with it. As the panel retracted into its compartment, her fingers were sliced off. Her head then hit the ceiling. Crushed, her scalp left a large inky stain that dripped down onto the floor. When the panel had completely retracted, she crumpled to the concrete, her legs splayed before her. The pawnshop owner hit the button once more. The transparent barrier fell, severing her legs.

No one inside the pawnshop moved. All of them, including the children, stared at the remains of the woman. Paul broke the silence. "Holy shit!" He gazed at the priest. "No offense, Father."

MacLeod sneered. "No offense? You said it before I could."

Openmouthed, Paul turned back to the woman.

The proprietor hit another button, and the protective panels separating him from the pawnshop rose. He made his way around the counter and stood with the others. Together they stared at the woman bleeding out on the floor.

"That was smart thinking," said Manuel, without taking his eyes off the woman. "Thank you, Mr. Jones."

The pawnshop owner didn't respond. The silence lingered.

It was short-lived.

Lynne whispered, "Oh my God." She pointed to the children.

They had stepped back from the barrier and were floating two feet off the floor, staring straight ahead. The barrier was distorted. Damaged. Small streams of clear fluid followed the surface downward, pooling onto the cement floor.

"The barrier is melting," Father MacLeod said, shaking his head. "They're melting the fucking thing."

The onlookers pulled back as a group, tight against the counter.

A pair of holes appeared in the panel. It continued to melt, the holes growing larger.

"Mr. Jones," cried Paul, "what can we do?"

The answer came, but not from the pawnshop owner.

"Nothing."

Irene's body was upright, resting on the stumps of her legs. Bones cracked as she lifted her head toward them. Her skull sat crooked on her broken neck. The darkness in her eyes and mouth spilled out in wisps.

"Weapons," the pawnshop owner said, "we need weapons." He ran behind the counter, going directly to a rack near the end. He retrieved a long box and slammed it onto the counter. Opening it, he removed a sheathed katana and placed it down. He reached in again and produced three more swords with colorful protective covers. All were shorter than the katana and of various widths. He removed the sheaths and handed the weapons to MacLeod, Paul, Lynne, and Manuel.

"Do these have any special powers that we should be aware of?" asked the priest.

The proprietor's answer was short. "No."

"Swords?" said Manuel. "Don't you have any guns? Something that will blow them apart?"

Lynne moaned. "My baby."

The proprietor's answer was the same. "No."

"What about you and Rex?" Paul asked the pawnshop owner.

"That's all I have. Rex will have to use his skills; I'll look for something else. Paul, Lynne, you two see if you can hold off the woman." He pointed at the children. "MacLeod, you and Manny take those two."

Lynne cried out, "No! That's my daughter!"

The pawnshop owner came around the counter and stood before her. "That is NOT your daughter. She's gone. The demon has claimed her." Softening his tone, he added, "And it will take us, too, maybe the entire world, if we don't stop it."

Sobbing, but trying to pull herself together, Lynne stood by Paul's side. Together they advanced toward the woman. Rex stayed close behind.

"He's right," claimed Irene as they approached her. "Your daughters' souls were lost to you the moment they were offered up to my master. He ate them. Chewed on their young and tender spirits. Their screams gave them strength as he swallowed their fear." She focused her empty eyes on Lynne. "He told me that Lisa's soul was particularly satisfying."

Shaking, Lynne stared at the woman, absorbing her taunts. The pawnshop owner was on the verge of shouting, telling her not to listen, that it was bait to get her to react. He was too late. A raw, screeching sound erupted from Lynne's throat. She lifted the sword, raising it above her head. Emitting a shriek that had Paul cowering, Lynne lunged at the woman. She closed her eyes and brought the sword down. Grief and anger flowed from her body into the killing blow, her screams now a heartbreaking wail. When the blade landed, her hands dropped from the sword on impact. Her upper body continued forward, the momentum too great to stop. Her torso hit the handle of the sword and she came to a jarring halt. Shaking off the pain, Lynne lifted her head and twisted it side to side. Moments later, she exhaled, lowered her chin, and opened her eyes.

Lynne winced. An inch above the woman's head, the sword was frozen in the air. Irene's palms were pressed flat against the blade, holding it in place.

"No," whimpered Lynne.

"Yes," hissed the woman. Leaning forward, Irene pushed the sword toward Lynne.

Its handle plunged into Lynne's chest. The pawnshop owner stood motionless as it exited through Lynne's back. He wasn't one to react emotionally when it came to death, but he could not deny the crushing weight in his heart as Lynne dropped to the floor convulsing.

"NO!" Paul dropped to Lynne's side. "Please, no, not you." Her eyes were opened wide. Blood bubbled and ran from her mouth. The blade quivered as her chest heaved. The gleaming metal stilled. Lynne was dead.

Rex stepped to the grieving man. He lifted Paul from the floor and walked him to the proprietor.

"Rex," the pawnshop owner said, his face hard, "destroy her." The giant nodded, but the proprietor saw something in the big man's face he had never seen before. Doubt. The expression was fleeting, replaced with stone-cold features, but it had been there. Rex swung his immense bulk toward the woman, fists clenched.

THIRTY

Father MacLeod's mind clouded as he watched Lynne take her last breath. While he didn't know the woman well, he thought her a good person, a loving mother. She didn't deserve this. If there was proof God didn't give a shit about the human race, her death would be exhibit number one. If what James Moore had told him was true, the devil had more reason than the Almighty to ensure the survival of mankind. The priest shook his head as Rex escorted Paul to the counter. *These are the people who deserve my respect, not some faceless man in the sky who's immune to our suffering.*

"Father," Manuel called to him. He placed a hand on his shoulder and asked, "Can you say a prayer to help us?"

MacLeod turned to the floating girls. The holes were much larger now, almost big enough for them to crawl through. "No, Manny. I think we're fucked."

Manuel blinked at the response.

"They'll be through any minute now," MacLeod said. Pointing to the sword, he asked, "You know how to use that thing?"

"No. How hard can it be?"

The priest sighed. "Ask Lynne."

When Manuel groaned, MacLeod followed up. "I'm sorry, but these demons have hellish strength and abilities. I'm not sure, but I think lifting the sword and bringing it down gives them enough time to react, even if it's only seconds. My guess is that we should be sticking it to them, fast and hard. Don't bring your arm back before you jab them, or they'll see it. Thrust, push the blade forward."

"You thought all that up just now?"

"Yeah."

"God *is* working through you, Father."

MacLeod frowned. "I doubt it."

Beneath the two holes, the melted portion of the barrier piled higher. The openings were almost large enough for the children to pass through. Moments later, they were. Arms outstretched and hands formed into claws, the two children floated forward.

"They're coming through!" shouted Manuel.

"You take the white girl." The priest swung his sword to his side, preparing to thrust it into the child's chest. When her hands broke through the opening, he stared into the child's eyes. He saw no shred of who she once was. Not a fragment of humanity shown through those misty black orbs. He was more than familiar with the possessed, especially children. Although there had been tense moments while exorcizing them, he did the job, and got it done. This was different. For the first time, he didn't think he was going to make it. Father MacLeod was afraid—afraid of a possessed child dragging him to Hell. All those demons he'd banished over the years would have a field day with him.

He stepped to the side and approached the barrier. Leaning against it, he brought the sword up high. He paused for a moment to ensure that enough of the child's arms were through the opening. After adjusting his stance to provide room and leverage, his arms tensed. The weapon dropped.

From the wrists down, two small hands landed on the piles of melted barrier.

Manuel was stunned. "Father, I thought you told me jab them."

The priest shrugged his shoulders. "I—I got scared. I couldn't let her get through. I had to do something."

Both girls flew back from the barrier. The one who called herself Cindy raised the stumps of her arms. Blood as black as coal gushed into the air, soaking her, the barrier, and her companion. MacLeod cringed, but he couldn't look away. The girl still floated, but she was motionless, staring at the stumps.

Something odd caught the priest's eye. Unsure of what it was, he leaned closer to the barrier. It was the blood spitting from the amputations. It was changing. The hue was lighter, resembling ash instead of charcoal. After a few more moments, the blood tinted red. *No!* MacLeod thought, *this can't be happening*. The red tint grew richer in color, turning deeper.

The girl's eyes blinked in slow motion. Each time they opened, the darkness residing in them receded. The sclera grew whiter with each blink. Her irises formed, the black fading to a dark brown. Her pupils regenerated, retaining the only hint of black. When the young girl's eyes were her own again, MacLeod knew only one thing remained foreign—the fright that radiated from them.

The reversion to her former self continued.

The darkness bled away from her open mouth. The priest could now see her pink tongue, teeth as white as new bed sheets, and lips a shade darker than her skin. Her lips moved. Though he couldn't hear her behind the barrier, he had no trouble deciphering the one word she uttered.

"Mom?"

The floating girl tumbled to the floor, flailing. Her accelerated heartbeat pumped the balance of blood from her stumps until it was reduced to a trickle. When the convulsions stopped, she lay on the floor, facing the counter. She repeated the single word she had uttered a moment earlier, after which, she stared ahead, her eyes wide, seeing nothing.

MacLeod fought off tears. The pawnshop owner was wrong. Those girls were still inside their bodies, hidden so deep no one knew they were there. *I just killed a young girl.* The thought was soul crushing, and he was paralyzed with grief.

"She said 'Mom.'"

MacLeod was so lost in thought he didn't realize Paul had left the counter and approached them. "Yes, she did, Paul. I feel so b—" It came to him. "Wait—"

Paul interrupted. Dazed, he spoke matter-of-factly. "It was Lisa inside her. Lisa called to her mother."

Manuel jumped in. "That means Cindy was never inside her." After a pause, he added, "Cindy might still be inside this one." He pointed to the remaining floating girl.

Paul choked back a sob. Staying to the side of the hole, he stepped closer to the barrier. He stared hard at the floating girl. "Cindy! Cindy, if you're in there, please, for the love of God, let me know."

MacLeod, still reeling, dropped the sword. He shook his head in an attempt to clear his thoughts. If Cindy were trapped inside, would an exorcism free her? Could Cindy give him her possessor's name? Would there even be an opportunity to perform the ritual? It was doubtful. From the din in the pawnshop, Rex was somewhere behind him, battling the woman. If Rex lost, chances were they were all fucked, anyway.

First things first, right now, this girl had to be reckoned with. If she came out of that hole and attacked them, who was going to stop her? Now that they knew Cindy was somewhere inside her, could Paul coax her to help them? There was nothing MacLeod could do to assist Rex, but maybe there was a chance he could help Paul.

"Paul, keep going. Try to reach her," he told him.

They made eye contact, and Paul nodded.

"Cindy," Paul pleaded, "I know you're in there. You've got to fight this! Please, it's me, Daddy. Come back to me, Cindy. Come back."

The girl floated without movement. Paul continued to implore her to return. After a few moments, the girl's head tilted to the side, studying Paul. "Keep going," MacLeod urged, "I think you're getting through."

Tears streaked Paul's face. "Please, Cindy. Come back and I'll take you home. I love you so much. I'll never leave you alone again. It will just be just the two of us. Come on, Cindy, baby, you can do it."

The girl's features went into motion. Like her companion, the darkness drifted from her eyes. Her mouth closed, and when it reopened, MacLeod could see her tongue. The transformation was rapid. When complete, the girl fell to the floor.

"Cindy!" Paul shouted. He bent to the hole.

The priest called to him. "Paul, wait. Give it a few moments. We have to make sure she's really back."

"She is back! Can't you see?" Paul sobbed. "My Cindy is back."

"Call her. Let her come to you," answered MacLeod.

Cindy blinked. A frown appeared. She sat up and gazed at her surroundings. Confused, she called for her father.

"I'm right here, Cindy. Come to me. Crawl through the hole, I'm here waiting for you."

The young girl's eyes lit up. "Daddy!" Placing her hands so she was on all fours, Cindy crawled through the hole. Before her legs were out, Paul grabbed the child and hugged her tight.

Father MacLeod exhaled. He fought back the rush of emotions overwhelming him. Though it galled him to say it, he muttered, "Thank you, God."

Paul hugged his daughter so tight, it was a wonder she could breathe. Finally, he pulled her back and gazed at her face. Holding her with one arm, he used the other to pat her head, running his fingers through her blond hair. "Oh, Cindy, I missed you so much."

MacLeod couldn't help noticing how beautiful the child's smile was.

She reached out to her father, placing both her hands on his shoulders, gripping him tightly.

"Daddy?" she said.

Paul returned the smile. "Yes, Cindy?"

"You're a fucking moron." Her hands went to his neck. She pushed with one hand and pulled with the other. MacLeod heard the snap as Paul's head swung violently to the right. Paul's eyes widened. As he dropped to the floor, they closed.

MacLeod stepped back. He knew he should say something, do something, but his body refused to respond. He could only watch as the girl crawled away from her father's corpse. She stood and faced MacLeod. Demonic features filtered back into her face. "It's your turn, priest. Oh, the fun we'll have with you in Hell."

MacLeod closed his eyes. The image of her deranged smile and darkening eyes were burned on his retinas. There was a snarl. He tensed, waiting for the girl to strike.

It never came.

He opened his eyes.

Manuel was standing several feet in front of him. The man held his sword out, blood dripped along its length. In front of Manuel, Cindy's body swayed. MacLeod's gaze went to the floor, where he saw the young girl's head.

Manuel broke the silence. "I—I..."

Whatever he was going to say, he never had a chance to finish.

"Look out!" The pawnshop owner's voice was loud enough to startle both of them.

MacLeod spun. Rex was flying through the air toward them.

THIRTY-ONE

The pawnshop owner could see MacLeod and Manuel squaring off against the children. He turned away. He would have to trust they could hold the kids off long enough for Rex to kill the woman. If Rex was unsuccessful, the two men's outcome wouldn't matter all that much. Judging from the fleeting look of doubt on the giant's face, the pawnshop owner was concerned. Rex might need help, and there was only one item in the shop that would be of assistance.

The Prexy Box.

If the proprietor could find a way to get the box close enough to the woman without her realizing it, its pull might be enough to give Rex the upper hand. What he didn't know was if the demon, the Dark Master she claimed to worship, also resided within her, or if it simply bestowed the abilities she possessed. If it was inside her, it would be one soul too many. The box could only deal with one at a time. If the Prexy Box took the woman's soul first and left the demon's, the box would be the demon's for the taking. The proprietor decided the risk was too great. Rex, left to his own devices, was their best chance of a favorable outcome.

Fists clenched, the giant barreled toward the woman. When he was within striking distance, she raised both fingerless hands, palms out, and pushed them toward Rex.

The pawnshop owner cringed. Rex's momentum came to a stop, his body flattening against an unseen wall. He grunted on impact and staggered back. He took a moment to collect himself, then stepped toward the woman. He glanced at the proprietor and tilted his head.

"It's not the pawnshop's," relayed the owner.

Rex nodded. He opened his hands, placed them on the invisible wall, and leaned in. Shifting his weight to his left foot, he drew back his right leg, planting his toes on the cement floor. He squared his shoulders and pushed.

Rex's arm muscles bulged as he applied pressure. His face tightened. Head lowered, he gritted his teeth as he pushed. It was working. By inches, he made headway.

The woman leaned forward, attempting to push back. Without legs to stand on, her body teetered on stumps. A groan spilled out as she focused her will against the giant. Her arms shook from the effort.

Sweat beaded on Rex's face. His groans grew louder as he pushed, drowning out the woman's. His palms were inches away from hers; he would close the gap in seconds.

Their palms never made contact. With a scream born from pain, the woman dropped her arms.

Rex shot forth like a bull released from its pen. He slammed into the woman, knocking her over as he sailed past. Though he landed on his face, the giant sprung to his feet and turned to her. Without pause, he lunged.

Palms out, the woman's arms flew back up. Rex collided with another invisible wall. He ricocheted off and was propelled head first into the pawnshop—his 400-plus pounds hurtling in the direction of Manuel and the priest. Rex angled his body, twisting it in an attempt to miss the two. He was partially successful. Most of his bulk avoided the men, but he sideswiped them as he rushed past. Father MacLeod was thrown against the barrier while Manuel tumbled backward onto the floor. Both were motionless.

Rex slammed against the protective barrier along the back wall, his head taking the brunt of the impact. On the floor, he glared at the woman.

The proprietor couldn't tell if Rex was injured or not. Moments later he had his answer.

Rex stood.

The giant's eyes were wild but focused on the woman. He opened his mouth wide enough to bare clenched teeth. The pawnshop owner knew that look. If Rex had doubts about destroying the woman, they had vanished. This was Rex at his most fierce, his most dangerous. For the first time today, the proprietor harbored hope.

The woman's arms were down by her sides, palms scraping the floor, but with her distorted features it was difficult to gauge her intentions. In an instant, that changed as she shot forward. She floated off the floor and charged Rex with the speed of a panther, knocking him down. Hands raised, she lowered them to his chest, and pressed with her palms.

Rex attempted to lift his arms, but they would only raise a few inches. He tried the same with his head, but his brow made contact with another of the woman's invisible walls. He struggled to throw her off, twisting his body in an attempt to get leverage with his legs. His efforts failed; wide-eyed, his chest compressed as her unseen barrier crushed him. The giant's lips puffed out as he expelled air.

There was only one thing left for the pawnshop owner to do. He pulled a stepstool from the end of the counter, placing it near the controls. He climbed to the top rung, moved a picture aside on the shelf, and removed the Prexy Box. Climbing down, he paused to see if he was too late. Rex's eyes were open, but barely. He stared at the proprietor, shaking his head. The pawnshop owner mouthed, "I have no choice." He rushed to the far end of the counter but halted when a low-pitched yell stopped him in his tracks.

"AHHHH, FUCK YOU!"

His head swung to the source.

Manuel stood to the side of the woman. Both his arms were raised high, holding the sword the pawnshop owner had given him. The weapon descended, rose, and fell again.

Her hands were sliced from her body. The invisible wall holding Rex vanished.

Father MacLeod stood off the floor and approached Manuel. "What happened to thrust and jab?"

"Well," said Manuel in defense, "it worked for you."

The priest shook his head. "Copycat."

Rex pushed the woman off and grabbed her arms. After ripping them from her sockets, he stomped them into a bloody pulp and tossed the mess into a corner.

Prexy Box in hand, the pawnshop owner joined the other three on the floor. All four of them formed a circle around the woman. The darkness in her eyes and mouth receded, her black blood now tinting red. It wasn't long before they all saw Irene as she had been before. Tears forming, she looked at each of them in turn. When she saw the priest, she said, "Do not weep for me."

"I had no plans to," answered MacLeod. "And how the fuck are you still alive?"

Irene ignored him. "Dark Master," she pleaded, "I need your help. Come for me."

The light in the pawnshop dimmed. By the front doors, a shadow formed. It grew darker, lengthening, widening until it obscured the entrance. The four of them left Irene and retreated to the counter.

They silently watched as the darkness deepened. When it was completely opaque, small tendrils of charcoal mist floated from it, surrounding its exterior. There was a ripple. On each side a pair of black waves pushed through.

Something stepped out between them.

THIRTY-TWO

Father MacLeod had encountered many demons during his exorcisms, but none of them projected the power of this one. Belphegor, the demon they had battled at the Moore House, was the closest. Though huge and powerful in its own right, Belphegor had the demeanor and appearance of a sixteenth-century inspired creature. It was slow, single-purposed, and feral. This demon, the Dark Master standing before them, had a human-shaped body with the physique of a superhuman It was taller than Rex, with muscles that put the giant to shame. It was naked, and if the inferences Manuel made about Irene coupling with this demon were true, MacLeod marveled that the woman had survived. Despite its enormity and physical prowess, it was the demon's eyes that held the priest's attention. Highlighted by its jet-black skin, its yellow orbs radiated intelligence and hate.

Its muscles rippling as it walked, the demon made its way to Irene.

Broken and lying in a pool of blood, the woman managed a weak smile. "You've come for me," she whispered.

"I am here," it answered.

"Heal me. I will stand by your side."

"No. I have no further use for you."

Irene's face tensed. Her voice faint, she said, "Bathin, I've done everything you asked to help you defeat Shaytan."

At the mention of the Dark Master's demon name, Father MacLeod's head swung to the pawnshop owner. The proprietor asked him, "Can you do anything with it?"

"I don't know if there's time. I need my book. Grab my things under the counter. But there's something else you should know."

The pawnshop owner was in motion, attempting to rush behind the counter and grab the priest's bag. "What?"

"She mentioned another demon's name. We may have more company."

The proprietor paused. "That second name. I've never heard of it. What the hell is it?"

A deafening roar filled the pawnshop before MacLeod could answer. Their attention went to the Dark Master, who had bent low over Irene.

Furious, the demon asked her, "How did you learn my name, woman?"

Blood dribbled from her mouth. She shuddered, and her face turned to the floor.

The demon dropped to his knees. "You bitch! Do you know what you have done?" Fists pounded into her face, beating her until her bones were splintered and mingled with blood. With a roar, it lifted its leg and plunged his foot into her torso.

"BATHIN!"

A chill went through the priest.

The company had arrived.

The Dark Master's head shot up.

MacLeod and the pawnshop owner turned to the source. Someone stood near the front doors. There was nothing extraordinary about its physique. It stood tall—its pose suggesting it was fit but not overly muscled. Naked, there was no doubt it was a male, but possessed nothing extraordinary.

From its skull to its feet, the demon's skin was deep red. Atop its bald pate were a pair of horns. Its most striking feature was a set of fully extended black wings that jutted four feet from either side of its back. MacLeod noticed its eyes were blue, like ice frozen over. He also took note of the demon's toes and hands. They, too, were human-like. The thought came to him that he shouldn't be surprised. This creature was once an angel.

The pawnshop owner leaned into the priest. "What are we looking at here?"

Without taking his eyes off the red demon, MacLeod answered, "It's Shaytan. You know him as Lucifer. He's the Devil himself."

Lucifer raised its hand, pointing to the two of them. "Leave the exorcism book..." it commanded in a voice with a slight echo to the words. It turned back to Bathin and added, "...you won't need it."

Bathin's eyes were ablaze. "You! How did you find me?"

"You *were* worthy of my admiration, Bathin," Lucifer answered. "Your power grew so great that my minions couldn't track you down. You've learned a lot while serving me. As powerful as you became, as smart as you think you are, you should have known I would find you. It was the woman. She reeked of you, and it was only a matter of time before she would lead me to you. Weak and easily susceptible, I knew she would betray you. With one visit, I tempered the gifts you bestowed upon her, and I made sure she would give you up. She could not die before she uttered both our names in your presence."

Enraged, Bathin roared. Bringing its arms up, it charged Lucifer.

The Devil shook its head, and Bathin froze like a statue.

Lucifer pointed to Father MacLeod. "You! Bring me the box."

The pawnshop owner spoke out, calmly, without fear. "I can't let him do that."

Lucifer laughed, its voice sending cold ripples down the priest's back.

"I could possess you and make you kill yourself," the Devil replied. Glaring at MacLeod, he added, "Maybe it would be fun to let the priest do it instead."

Neither man spoke.

"I know the abilities of the box," Lucifer continued. "This may surprise you, but I am pleased it exists and you have ownership. Those souls are already mine; you are merely their caretaker. Consider them my reserves. I may have need for them someday if the balance of power between your God and my kingdom shifts. As of now, there is no need to upend the dynamics. There is plenty of fresh fruit to pick here and keep me satiated. I give you my word, I will not take possession of the box, at least at this time."

The pawnshop owner asked the priest, "Can I believe it?"

"It's the fucking Devil! How am I supposed to know?" MacLeod thought for a few seconds. "If it's telling the truth, maybe we can get something out of this."

"Are you nuts? You want to make a deal with the Devil?"

"Yeah."

Father MacLeod turned to Lucifer. "If we do this for you, we are taking one hell of a chance. In the name of fairness, I would like you to do something for me."

Once more, the Devil's laugh echoed through the pawnshop. "You have some big balls, priest. What is it you want?"

"I'd like a 'Get Out of Hell' card."

The pawnshop owner groaned. "Can't you ever think of anyone else but yourself?"

Lucifer did not laugh at the request. "No. Your soul is mine, and you still owe me one. You and your God are the only ones who can change that. And, from what I know of you and Him, you will stay mine."

The priest sighed. "Doesn't hurt to ask. How about something else, then? My colleague, Celeste, is currently in limbo while keeping a leash on one of your more recent demonic graduates. Its name is James Moore. How about you bringing Moore back to Hell and keeping it there? Celeste is not one of yours and she never will be. She belongs back here with us."

Lucifer grinned. "There is no need for me to do anything for any of you here, certainly not you, priest. But, as you might know, I enjoy making deals, and you have presented me a unique challenge. I will reclaim James Moore and confine him. I will leave the box in the possession of its current owner. You have my word. Now bring the box to me."

The pawnshop owner was deep in thought when MacLeod asked him for the box.

"Look," the priest said, "we don't have any choices here. Let's do this now and get it over with."

"You're right," said the proprietor, "it's not like I have a choice." He removed the Prexy Box from the counter and handed it to the priest. MacLeod took it and approached Lucifer. The demon flinched when the priest came near and took a step back. The priest noticed the reaction and set the box down on the floor between the two demons. He hoped the pawnshop owner had missed the Devil's expression.

Wearing an uneasy look, Lucifer bent over to pick the box up. It studied the box for a few moments. "I cannot see into the box."

The pawnshop owner spoke up. "Maybe, it's because you are not the current owner."

Remaining silent for a moment, Lucifer finally spoke. "This is interesting." He glanced at the priest for a moment and then said to the pawnshop owner, "It appears you people are full of surprises. Do what you do, human."

The pawnshop owner went to Rex, who was sitting at the far end of the wall. He was awake, but his expression made it difficult to determine if fully. Manuel stood by Rex's side, his hand on the giant's shoulder.

"Rex, you still with us?"

The giant made eye contact with the proprietor. He nodded.

"I need you to operate the Prexy Box. You up to it?"

With another nod, Rex stood. He walked over to Bathin. The giant motioned for Lucifer to stand back, and it complied. Rex faced the frozen demon. With the fiery eyes of a madman, the giant reared one arm back and plunged it forward into the Dark Master's chest. The demon remained statuesque, exhibiting no pain. Rex shifted his hand inside the demon's torso until he found what he was looking for. When he withdrew his hand, it held Bathin's black heart. Bending to his knees, the giant placed the organ near the top of the Prexy Box. Tendrils of dark smoke emanated from the heart, forming a silhouette of the demon. A moment later, Bathin's essence was vacuumed into the Prexy Box. When the procedure was over, the giant turned to the pawnshop owner. The proprietor nodded. Rex brought the heart to his mouth, and he chewed.

"Holy shit," said MacLeod, "is that part of the procedure?"

"No," replied the pawnshop owner.

A sound like glass cracking enveloped the pawnshop. Spiderweb-like fissures appeared across Bathin's body. Still eating his meal, Rex moved away.

The demon's body fell to the floor in thousands of crystalline pieces.

Lucifer ignored Bathin's destruction and focused on Rex. "I like you. I hope someday you will serve at my feet."

Finishing his meal, the giant didn't bother to glance at the Devil when he said, "Fuck you."

The demon smiled. "I like you even more, now."

Lucifer approached the pawnshop owner. "Take care of that box. Those who reside in it *are* mine. Someday, I might have need of them."

The proprietor offered no response.

Facing MacLeod, Lucifer said, "There is something different about you. I need to discover what that is. In the meantime, arrangements have been made. James Moore is back in my kingdom. Your colleague is free to return to you. Regarding her, you have presented me with a challenge, and I look forward to it. As for you, priest, I will see you in Hell."

The Devil vanished.

The pawnshop owner wasted no time in collecting the Prexy Box. He rushed behind the counter and placed it on its shelf.

A commotion at the front of the shop drew his attention.

A crowd of people stood in the street. They milled about the damaged doors, pointing and calling to those inside asking if everyone was all right.

Father MacLeod watched the people through the doors. The small crowd vanished. The priest blinked in confusion. A moment later, the front of the pawnshop was back in order.

The doors were fixed, the debris gone. Everything was the same as it had been when he had first stepped into the shop. Two things were different, however. The view outside the doors had changed. Instead of the parking lot of the local hardware store, the priest saw a road, the far side covered in a thick copse of trees and brush. The other thing he saw was a human head, on the floor in the doorway. It was badly damaged. All of the skin was gone with the exception of a set of eyes that stared back at him. When he drew closer to it, the eyes followed his movements. A voice behind him spoke, and the priest jumped.

"When the demon-woman outside was looking in at us, she was holding a skull. I'm assuming this was that skull," said the proprietor.

"Yeah, but I think it's still alive! How is that possible?"

"I don't know."

Manuel had come to the front of the shop to join them. "If I were to guess, I'd say it's Donald, Irene's husband. It's tough to tell, though, with it looking like that. What are you going to do with it?"

"Again, I don't know. I'll store it someplace, try to find a way to put it out of its misery, if that's possible."

MacLeod pointed to the entrance of the shop. "What's with that? It's all fixed. And what the hell happened to the hardware store?

While examining the skull, the proprietor casually explained, "The pawnshop takes care of itself. It moves to new locations when the necessity arises."

"Wait. You mean the whole shop just pulls up stakes and moves somewhere else? Where the hell are we now?"

The proprietor frowned. "I am tired of answering your questions. We are still in Goffstown. The shop never moves outside the town's limits."

Manuel interrupted. "We still have a problem we're going to have to address." He pointed to the bodies of Paul, Lynne, Irene, and the two children. "What are we going to do about them?"

"Rex and I will take care of them."

"But..."

The pawnshop owner placed his hand on Manuel's shoulder. "I said we would take care of them. We will be respectful, and make sure Irene's death is not connected to you."

Father MacLeod smiled and threw his hands up. "Well, it sounds like you got everything under control. Nice! Now if I can figure out where I am and how to get to my car, I'll be out of here."

The pawnshop owner maneuvered himself in front of the priest. "Not so fast."

MacLeod sighed. He knew what was coming.

"Give me the necklace."

"Necklace? I told you I—"

"We saw what happened to them when you were in the proximity of Irene and Lucifer, so stop lying." The pawnshop owner paused. "Rex, would you be so kind as to retrieve my property from this man?"

MacLeod's eyes widened. "No. No." He reached into his back pocket and handed it over. "You can't blame me for trying, can you?"

The proprietor placed the necklace into his own pocket. "Please leave. I hope to never see you again."

MacLeod grinned. "Same here." He waved as he walked to the front door and said, "So long, everybody—" Rex took a step toward him before he could finish the sentence.

Rushing out the door, the priest didn't look back.

THIRTY-THREE

Positioned behind one of the pawnshop's protective barriers, the shew-stone had been spared any damage during the encounter with the demons the day before. The proprietor ran his fingers over the smooth surface. As morning light illuminated the stone, he wondered why it had been considered a failure in its time. Though it didn't provide a whole lot of information when presented with the question pressed against it, what it did show them was somewhat, if not precisely, accurate. Maybe the future could be altered, or at least tweaked. He made a mental note to do more research on this stone and learn as much of the *enochian script* as possible.

A sharp beep alerted the proprietor that someone was at the front doors. His back stiffened. He had made the decision that morning to open up the shop and let some air in. It reeked of death. After sending Manuel home the previous evening, Rex had assisted with the removal of the bodies. The two of them had set up scenarios that would lead investigators to conclude that the dead were victims of accidents or arson. The fires were intense—they needed to be in order to reduce the bodies to ash. Sirens had wailed through the night, but he and Rex had stayed ahead of them, or so he thought. The pawnshop owner was tired, and the last thing he wanted right now was to be answering questions from authorizes or chasing out nosey customers. Remaining by the stone, he glanced toward the doors. The visitor addressed him.

"You look pretty good for someone who danced with the Devil yesterday."

The proprietor grinned. "I could say the same for you."

The two stood, each taking the other in.

"Celeste, I'm so glad you are back with us. You look wonderful, no worse for wear."

She walked into the pawnshop and he left the stone to greet her. They embraced; her head fell on his shoulder and it remained there for several heartbeats. "Thank you," she said, then added, "it's good to be back."

Celeste broke the embrace and stepped back. "You know, you never told me your name."

"Names have power. I have guarded mine for a long time. It's not that I don't trust you, Celeste, but people can be made to give up secrets. If my name is important to you, try calling me Mr. Smith."

She shook her head. "No, that won't do. You see, I've had a long time to think about you. About us. To put it mildly, I'm quite fond of you. If I'm not mistaken, I think you feel the same about me."

The pawnshop owner lowered his head. "It's been a long time since I've had a woman friend. Not only has my work kept me busy, but as you know, it can be quite dangerous. I have serious reservations about letting someone into my life who might get hurt."

Celeste's face dropped. "I—I understand."

"However, you are correct. I have become quite fond of you. Also, you've been through Hell and back. You fully understand the risks and dangers of my profession. You have abilities that can protect you if things get bad. If I were to choose someone to be with, I couldn't think of a better woman than you."

Her face lit up. "Does that mean—?"

The pawnshop owner smiled. "Celeste, are you free for dinner this evening?"

She fell back into his arms and held him tight.

He placed his hands on her hips and gently pushed her away. "Two things. First, you can't be calling me, Mr. Smith. Pick a name, and I will answer to it."

"Gabriel."

His head reared back. "That was fast."

"No, not really. You forget, I had a long time to think. What's the second thing?"

The pawnshop owner reached into his back pocket. "Remember this?"

Her mouth opened. "The necklace. How could I forget?"

"I want you to wear this, always. Never take it off, Celeste. Ever. MacLeod might be the reason you came back to us, but the terms of his bargain with the devil may carry peril for you. The priest mentioned something about you never belonging to Lucifer, and Lucifer might have taken MacLeod's words as a *challenge*."

He handed her the necklace and she placed it around her neck. "I don't understand, Gabriel. What happened?"

Inwardly, he winced when she called him by that name. The feeling passed and he reached for her hand. "I'll tell you at dinner this evening. What do you say, six o'clock?"

Celeste nodded. "That gives me time to get back to Haverhill and get ready. I'll meet you here if that's okay."

"It's perfect."

She left his side and walked to the door but stopped short. "We have a lot to discuss this evening. I'm not sure there will be enough time to go over everything. I'm going to book a room at the Holiday Inn in Manchester. Is that okay with you?"

The pawnshop owner nodded. "It's more than okay."

Tony Tremblay is the author of the novel **The Moore House**, which was a finalist for the Bram Stoker award. He has also authored two collections, **The Seeds of Nightmares**, and **Blue Stars and Other Tales of Darkness**. His short stories have appeared in numerous anthologies in the US and across the pond.

Tony was host of *The Taco Society Presents,* a genre television interview show, and is co-editor of the anthologies **Fright Train** (with Charles R. Rutledge and Scott Goudsward), and **Eulogies II** and **Eulogies III** (with Nanci Kalanta and Christopher Jones). He is a co-founder of *NoCon*, a yearly genre convention held in Manchester, NH. Tony was a former reviewer for the *Horror World* website, *Cemetery Dance Magazine*, and *Beware the Dark* magazine.

Tony lives in New Hampshire with his wife.

You can visit Tony at TonyTremblayAuthor.com or visit him on Facebook.